Dangerous

The Finn Factor, Book 3

Free Read:

A Curious Proposal

(An Owen and Jeremy Quickie)

Natalie, Enjoy!

RG Alex

R.G. ALEXANDER

DEDICATION

Cookie—Love is the reason. Robin—you will always be my diamond. Readers…You've been so patient and so caring, I really hope you love Brady and Ken and enjoy meeting the rest of the Finn family!

CHAPTER ONE

"Are all Marines this lazy in the morning?"

The amused male voice in Brady Finn's ear sounded familiar, but he didn't have a chance to wonder why or respond to the question. As soon as he tried to move, his head began to throb so violently it felt like it was preparing to rip itself off his body. He almost wished it would. "Oh God."

He lowered his arms from their position over his head and dragged his palms slowly down his face, willing his brain to function and the tips of his hair to stop hurting. Why the hell did his *hair* hurt?

The pub. He'd been at the pub. He'd had a drink and played a game of darts with his cousin Seamus, listening to his renovation plans for the bar and trying not to think about where he was going to go now that he'd left Owen and Jeremy's guest room. Of course then Owen had surprised him by showing up to talk and buying him another round of what he'd been drinking.

Rum. He remembered the rum.

Now every cell in his body was rebelling against him and he was in a strange bed with no memory of what he'd done last night after he got halfway through the second bottle.

The body beside him shifted and he rethought that last statement. He had no memory of *who* he'd done last night. Shit.

Brady carefully squinted against the brightness of the bedroom. At first all he could see through his lashes was a smile—gleaming white teeth framed by lips that were made for every wicked thing a man could imagine. He would know that mouth anywhere.

It belonged to Kenneth Tanaka.

Maybe he was still asleep. The pain was reminiscent of one of his nightmares, but the scenes that haunted him didn't usually include waking up beside a man he'd lusted after for months. That was a completely different type of torture.

It couldn't be Tanaka. Brady hadn't seen the

tempting computer hacker in nearly five weeks. Not since Stephen's wedding reception. He'd had a little to drink that night too, but he remembered every second of their last encounter, and the vow he'd made the next morning not to finish what he'd started with the kinky bastard. No matter how much he wanted to.

The soft laugh sounded like loud, angry bells to his sensitive ears. "You're not looking so good, Finn. Rough night?"

It *was* him. *Son of a bitch.*

"Water," Brady rasped, his throat raw and dry and his need to delay a morning-after conversation paramount in his mind. "I need water."

All of it. He needed every drop the man could find. And then, when he was hydrated enough to move, he was planning on throwing up, hopefully in private, preferably in a seedy motel where no one would think to look for him and he could suffer in peace.

The bed bounced lightly when Ken rolled off and Brady groaned. "I'm dying."

"Sit up first. I brought you something to drink."

Water? His movements were clumsy and leaden as he twisted so he could plant his feet on the smooth wood floor. He stifled another groan and rested his aching head in his rough, wide palms. "I don't get hangovers. I never get hangovers."

His brothers always said he had the constitution of an ox. Specifically Babe the Blue Ox—because giant references never got old in his family. It was a challenge to get him tipsy, and he'd never gotten so hammered he blacked out. He left that to the more adventurous Finns.

Speaking of his drinking buddy… "Owen?"

"Your cousin is fine," Ken assured him wryly. "It's barely eleven-thirty and he's already called your phone five times." He took one of Brady's hands in his and wrapped his fingers around a hot cup. "And he's not the only one who called and left a message. Don't drop that—drink it so you can tell them the bad man didn't leave you in a tub of ice without your kidneys."

Eleven-thirty? How had he slept so long?

You got drunk and passed out. Keep up, moron.

"Keep your voice down," he grumbled at Ken and the voice in his head. "At least until the room stops spinning."

Ken lowered his voice obediently. "This should help."

Brady managed to raise his head enough to study the steaming cup in his hand. The brown liquid smelled like

4

cloying incense and wet burlap. Definitely not water. "What is it?" he asked suspiciously. "Poison?"

"This is the antidote. You've never had a hangover? Well I've never had a naked man get sick in my bed. I like this bed and when I'm in it I like thinking about healthy naked men. So drink. All of it."

Brady gulped it down without another word, willing to do whatever it took to find relief while he adjusted to the reality of his situation. The task would be easier if he knew where his clothes were.

Had he and Tanaka…? No. He would have remembered that. God, what if he didn't remember that?

The flavor was worse than the smell. Brady grimaced and choked when he reached the dregs at the bottom. "This tastes like swamp and shame."

Tanaka removed the cup from his white-knuckled grasp and set it down beside the bed. "That means it's working. It's my recipe for demon cleansing. Foul, but it usually does the trick. Of course I've never been stupid enough to down three bottles of rum in one night, so I make no guarantees, but in a few minutes you should feel like a new man. You might even thank me."

Three bottles? It was a miracle he wasn't in the ER. Right now he would give just about anything to be a new man. One who didn't have to wonder whether or not he had something to apologize for. "Thanks."

"Damn, I'm good. It's working already."

"Smartass." Brady took a bracing breath and looked up into the face that had starred in all his fantasies for the last few months. More beautiful than handsome, Ken Tanaka had the kind of looks that no one, male or female, would be able to ignore.

He was shirtless—a state he seemed to prefer—and his smooth honeyed skin stretched tight over all his lean muscle. Brady's fingers twitched with the need to reach out and touch him, to trace the tattoo that trailed down Ken's right arm and, Brady knew, completely covered his back. To wrap his fingers around the waist-length, midnight-black braid that was falling over one shoulder like heavy silk.

His gaze returned to Tanaka's face so he wouldn't be tempted to linger below his well-defined stomach muscles and realized that Ken was shamelessly returning the favor. Thickly lashed eyes, which changed in hue from dark amber to molten gold, were studying Brady's body in a way that made him keenly aware of the fact that there was nothing but a thin sheet draped over his lap. A drape that was quickly morphing into a tent to house his growing erection.

Classy, Finn.

At least one part of his body still worked. At this point he'd take any silver lining he could find, including the fact that Ken was wearing pants.

But how long had they been on? Brady refused to believe he'd ever forget a naked Ken Tanaka. Just the thought of the man without any clothing was enough to heighten his arousal.

"I don't remember much about last night…" he started, letting his voice trail off as he tried to casually shift enough to conceal his hard-on.

"Hold that thought. Let me get you that glass of water."

Brady closed his eyes, grateful for the momentary reprieve. *Think of water*, he told himself. *Ice. Antarctica.* He needed to nip this in the bud before it got out of hand, because at some point he was going to have to leave this bed and find his clothes and a bathroom, and he'd prefer not to prove how little control he had around Tanaka.

At the sound of light footsteps and tinkling ice, he opened his eyes and accepted the glass Ken handed him. "Thank you."

"Define much," Ken ordered with narrowed eyes.

Brady took a long, careful sip before saying, "Well, I don't know how I got here."

"In my car. You were in no shape to drive your motorcycle."

When Ken didn't offer any further clues, Brady said pointedly, "I'm also not sure where my clothes are."

"The ones you were wearing are in the dryer. The rest are still packed, I imagine."

Brady frowned. Was Ken being vague on purpose? Was he having fun at his expense or just trying to find the right way to tell him exactly how out of line he'd been?

Struggling to fill in the blanks himself, he said, "I was talking to Owen. He wanted my advice about Jeremy. I remember *that* clearly because I couldn't get over the fact that he was finally asking."

"Oh, I know. It was obvious you had a lot to say on the subject," Ken said, sitting down beside him with a glint in his eyes.

Brady almost choked on his next sip of water. "You were there?"

"Not for the live performance, no. But I did watch the replay."

Live performance? Replay? "I don't understand."

"It might be easier to swallow if I tell you a story. Once upon a time, some idiot at a bar thought it would be fun to record his friends getting drunk. When a conversation between two tipsy Irishmen got everyone's attention, he trained his camera on them. It was so good he uploaded it to YouTube, sure it would be more popular than the Instagram account he'd made for his cats."

"You're fucking with me." Brady was horrified.

Ken shook his head and revealed the phone in his hand. "I'm not. I have it queued up right here."

He touched the screen and a smaller version of Brady appeared. His short red hair was mussed and his cheeks were ruddy with drink as he leaned against the bar and lectured the handsome blond beside him. The memories started coming back while he watched it unfold.

"You wanted my opinion, Owen, so listen up. What you have to do is *admit that you're gay*. The family pub is as good a place as any to start. Go on. Out loud so the whole class can hear you."

Nearby patrons instantly started pounding their tables in agreement with Brady.

"Say it," someone shouted.

"Loud and proud!" another replied with glee.

Owen looked around the sparsely populated bar before glaring at Brady. "What's it going to take before everyone stops giving me shit about this? Should I take out an ad in the paper or slap a rainbow sticker on my bumper?"

"Your mother has one," Brady countered. "But even after the happiest year of your life—your words—you haven't even considered it. Why?"

"No one has the right to stamp a label on me."

Brady rolled his eyes. "So you were fine with the man-whore, sex addict and lady killer labels? Good with all the other names women called you after they realized you weren't staying for breakfast or calling for a second date?"

The women in the pub booed playfully and Owen winced.

"The label isn't the point, dumbass," Brady continued. "But if you don't want it? Stop earning it. Your house has thin walls, and I rarely sleep as it is. I know what happens in your room every night. Everyone in a three-mile radius knows."

Several men in the bar groaned in protest, but Brady

just raised his voice. "I'm not exaggerating. I spent months wondering how either of them could walk without crutches. At least they have good health insurance. Can't say for sure that it covers their style of sexual acrobatics, but who knows?"

"Jealousy is an ugly emotion, cousin." A muscle twitched along Owen's jaw. Brady could see it clearly on the small screen. "Just because you're living like a monk doesn't mean the rest of us have to."

"Of course m'jealous," Brady's words were slurring, so he took another drink. "Anyone in this bar that says they're not is lying. Do you think I'm a monk by choice? I'm not. I miss sex. You have *no idea* how much I miss sex. I'd gladly risk regular trips to the hospital for exhaustion if I could have what you and Jeremy have. But we're not talking about my relationship issues; we're talking about yours. And when it comes to that, you, my friend, are spoiled. You hit the boyfriend jackpot and you got used to having all his time and energy. But as soon as he wasn't focused on you twenty-four hours a day you started acting like a petulant child."

"I'm not spoiled."

"Really? Who was the guy frowning in all your brother's wedding pictures because your boyfriend was

Man of Honor and had to help the bride instead of dance with you all night?"

Owen pointed at Brady. "That's not—"

"Who sat in his pajamas, eating pizza and pouting while I power-washed the dock and fixed the roof when Jeremy went to that convention last month and didn't invite you?"

Owen was scowling. "You said you didn't need help, and those comic book conventions are full of signature-starved deviants. I would be stupid *not* to worry about him going alone." He looked at the stranger next to him. "It's more complicated than he's making it sound. I'm not jealous of—"

"Right. You're not jealous," Brady interrupted, on a roll. "Because you're not gay and you two are just buddies. Buddies who fuck like it's an Olympic sport you're training to medal in. Who cuddle on the couch after work to watch a movie or slash your mutual Xbox enemies. Buddies who can't resist saying, 'I love you' and stopping to kiss every five minutes. When you're not holding hands and romping with your cute little dog by the lake."

A woman wearing a birthday tiara leaned on her hand and sighed beside them. "That sounds like heaven or a

Hallmark movie. If you don't want your boyfriend, Blondie, I'll take him off your hands. I love a good romp."

"*I want him.*" Owen covered his face with one hand, swearing before he turned back to the bar. "You're just trying to piss me off now."

Seamus moved into the camera's view. "Maybe you should give him a break, Brady."

"He doesn't need a break, he needs honesty. I'm actually trying to help." Brady laid a hand on Owen's shoulder and the image zoomed in. If he weren't so humiliated, he would have been impressed with the picture and sound quality on that asshole's smartphone.

"I get it, believe me," video-Brady rambled on. "Sure, with the family and at that private club of yours it's fine. But the same guys who praised you in the locker room for your football skills and lady-killer rep are avoiding you. You had one employee turn in his resignation when he found out. You stop yourself from kissing the man you love in public because you know people will stare. We can toast Ireland and the Supreme Court's decision all night long—" The pub cheered at that before he continued. "But we'll still have to wake up in the morning and know that people don't change as fast as the laws, and someone at the next party you go to will be surprised you don't act the way their favorite television show told them a gay man would."

"Exactly." Owen turned back to Brady, his own cheeks rosy with drink. "That's it, that's exactly it. It's none of their fucking business, is it? I'm in love with *Jeremy*. He's the only one I have to answer to. The only one that matters."

"Then why did you follow me here instead of talking to him?"

"I can't. Not about… I can't."

"You have to. Put yourself in his shoes for a minute. You won't say you're gay but you're still in his bed. I've seen the way he reacts. I know it bugs him. He's smart enough to know your kind of situation rarely turns out well. Loving him has made your life more difficult. He has to carry that, wondering each day if you're going to look at him and decide it's not worth it."

"Of course it's worth it. We already dealt with his doubts. He *knows* I love him. He knows I'm committed."

Brady scoffed. "I know he's gotten you to open up more than anyone else ever has, but you always hold something back. Like the fact that you've wanted to propose since you moved in."

Owen stared at him in telling silence.

"I'm right, aren't I? You've been too afraid to ask because you can't drag him to the altar the way you strong-armed your way into his pants and his house. He actually has to say yes to more than a shared pet and that is scaring the shit out of you. That's why you've been pissed every time his phone rings. Why I knew it was time to pack up this morning. You want to pop the question."

Owen was evasive. "I didn't mean to make you feel unwelcome, I just thought... I don't want to mess this up. If I'm doing it, it has to be right. And I need to have his undivided attention."

"Well, then take him to some romantic getaway where none of our relatives or his friends from the convention can get ahold of him. He'll say yes. He would've said yes a year ago." Brady paused and pounded the bar for emphasis. "But if you're serious, be serious. You're a Finn. We go all in or not at all. Don't use this bullshit label excuse anymore, because honestly? It sounds like you're keeping one foot out the door. Also, cool it with the jealous fishwife routine. You want to remind him of all the reasons he can't live without you, not send him running in the other direction."

"He won't be able to run." The smile on his cousin's face was disturbing. "Or answer his damn phone. I have a set of handcuffs and a paddle I can use that will make him agree to anything. Eventually."

The crowd at the bar cheered raucously and the camera focused on Brady's grimace before he reached for yet another drink of rum.

The woman in the tiara patted him on the shoulder, a wad of cash in her hand. "I always knew Cupid was a kinky redhead."

"I'm not kinky."

"Whatever. Now that you've solved his problem I have one that needs fixing. My friends hired a dancer for my birthday, but he didn't show up and Seamus refuses to show me his shameless side. Take it off, Red. Take it *all* off!"

The screen froze after that and Brady closed his eyes in humiliation. "So that really happened. I suppose it's lucky I don't have a lease and my passport's still good. I can be out of the country by tomorrow."

Ken laughed and set his phone down. "Relax, Cupid. It only had a couple of views before I scrubbed it and closed that idiot's account. He won't be uploading anything for a while. Neither will his cats. I did save a copy for myself since I missed seeing it in person by mere minutes."

And *that* was why he'd been drinking so heavily. He remembered—Ken had sent him a text message a few minutes before his cousin arrived, telling him to stay at the pub because they needed to talk. Had they had a conversation? Was there a video of that too?

Ken nudged his shoulder with his own. "No need to be embarrassed, Finn. That was an Academy-worthy speech, and long overdue. Owen can't stay in his bubble forever. You could be the spokesperson for the LGBT community. The new slogan would be 'Admit you're gay, everyone else knows anyway.'"

"Fuck you."

"Seriously, you're a surprisingly eloquent drunk. And a talented stripper."

His throat closed in panic. "Tanaka, I swear—"

"Kidding," Ken interrupted, laying a hand on Brady's biceps. "I'm kidding. I couldn't resist. But you can. Even when I offered to pay every tab at the bar and people were chanting your name in their bid for free beer, you wouldn't agree to stripping in public."

"Thank God for that." Brady realized abruptly that his head had stopped pounding. "And thank you for pulling that video down. I don't think I would've been welcome back for the holidays if anyone in the family had seen it. Seamus and Owen still might ban me for life after that performance." What had he been thinking?

Ken was caressing his arm now, a comforting, almost absent gesture that sent a blast of focused heat down his spine and straight to his cock. It was making it hard for Brady to breathe, but he couldn't force himself to move away.

"Seamus won't admit it," Ken said, "but he got a kick out of you reading the riot act to Owen. His twin might be a stuffy politician, but our bartender has a wild side. He's just too busy being Super Dad to let it out."

Brady grinned wryly. "Stephen isn't that stuffy."

"I am well aware." Ken's voice was a seduction. "I've seen Tasha in action at the club for years, and for weeks I've been seeing her glowing newlywed smile and their PDAs in the paper. No true vanilla could keep up with that sassy switch and make her as happy as he does."

Brady tensed in reaction and Ken's hand fell away. "I don't think I'm recovered enough to think about what my cousin can or can't keep up with. And you know I had my fill of BDSM buzz words at Burke's kinky party of the damned. I wanted to bleach my brain for weeks to forget it all—including the fact that vanilla refers to something other than a cool, delicious flavor of ice cream."

"You wanted to forget everything?"

Brady looked down at his hands. Not *everything*, but he wasn't recovered enough to think about that either.

It had been a strange experience. Playing Senator Stephen Finn's bodyguard for the federal investigation into Burke's illegal activities was a little too eye-opening for Brady's peace of mind. At least the sight of naked men voluntarily being strapped to crosses and women wagging their furry tails as they drank from a dish on the floor had shocked him out of his own head. He would be grateful if he could stop cringing every time he thought about it.

Kink was *not* his scene.

It was, however, Ken's. Seeing him at Burke's house, watching the way everyone looked to him for approval and how expertly he worked those ropes, had made it clear he was in his element.

It had also gotten Brady so hard he'd had to walk

away more than once to recover his composure. The one time he couldn't, Ken had kissed him, and it had been better than the best sex he'd ever had—which was sad when he let himself think about it.

But not even the intense chemistry between them would get Brady to date a man who considered pain and bondage a form of foreplay. Being tied up wasn't sexy; it was a training exercise in surviving interrogation and torture.

Brady still had no idea what had happened after his pub speech. A smart man wouldn't ask. A smart man would find his clothes and leave as fast as his hangover would let him.

Brady clearly wasn't that smart.

He turned his head to stare into golden eyes that were far too close for comfort. "Why am I here, Tanaka? Tell me the truth."

Ken's gaze dropped to his mouth. "Truth? You're here because Seamus is an easy mark, so the room behind the pub—the room Jen stayed in until she went back to college—is occupied for the next two weeks. Knowing him, it's probably another damsel in distress. Let's just hope she doesn't have a child in need of adopting. Seamus already has a full house."

He vaguely recalled it now. Seamus felt so guilty for not being able to help Brady right away that he'd offered him a drink on the house. And then another.

"Since you couldn't crash there, you had to start thinking about other options. You told me about your situation and I offered you a place to stay in exchange for your services."

And Brady had agreed? To *live* with Ken? He'd actually thought that was a good idea? Talk about impaired decision-making skills.

"You didn't have to do that." Brady gathered the sheet and stood up, away from temptation. "I have options. A few of them include couches I can sleep on free of charge until I find a place of my own."

Ken stood as he did, his arms crossed over his bare chest, drawing Brady's gaze to the silver cross that hung from an overlong chain around his neck. Had he seen that before? He didn't think so.

"I know about your options, Finn. Five brothers and a father who'd all be willing to let you stay with them as long as you started acting like yourself again and rejoined the police force. As long as you told exciting war stories while pretending your years in the military hadn't changed you."

"Wow." Brady ran his free hand through his hair, clutching the sheet with the other. "I *do* talk a lot when I'm drunk. And you were nice enough to give me a ride anyway. Sorry about that."

Ken's expression was intimate. "I'm not. Last night was unforgettable. For some of us. And I was already planning on asking for your help. We make a good team."

That was true enough. They'd toppled the corrupt Burke and the complicit local paper that was a part of his media empire. They'd also saved Seamus from losing Little Sean and gotten Tasha and Stephen back together, though Brady knew that most of it was Ken's doing. He was just the muscle who did good legwork. Tanaka had been the brain.

"So…you want me for a job? That's why I spent the night? You and I—we didn't…"

Ken's eyes sparkled with humor. "I was wondering when you'd get around to asking."

He strode up to Brady and gripped a handful of sheet in both hands and twisted so it tightened around his hips. He could feel the heat from Ken's body wrapping around him just as tightly. Holding him captive. "You don't remember the things you admitted to? The things you offered? Nothing?"

Brady swallowed hard. Hell. "No."

Ken whistled, drawing Brady's attention to his pursed lips. "Too bad. What you said made it nearly impossible for me not to pick up where we left off the last time I saw you. And when you asked me to help take off your clothes—"

"Damn it, Tanaka." Brady grabbed one of Ken's wrists in rough warning. "Don't dick around."

Bad choice of words. Ken's bringing up the last time they saw each other only made his current state of arousal harder to ignore.

Ken on his knees, sucking your cock.

Brady's fingers flexed in memory and Ken bit his lip. "Mmm, I do love that strong grip of yours. Brings back memories. You know, if you weren't so disgusted by kink I might think we shared an interest in noncon, but sadly, you are as vanilla as a gay Irish Marine can be."

Brady dropped his wrist a little too quickly. "What the hell is noncon?"

Refusing to release him, Ken gave him the kind of smile Lucifer must have worn the moment before he fell. "Consensual non-consent, Finn. A little game where one of us pretends to resist while the other forces us to take it. To love it." He licked his lips and Brady suppressed another shiver of awareness. "Shame, really. You're big enough to be a challenge and I have a thing for muscle-bound gingers who talk too much when they drink."

Damn. "Tanaka—"

"Yes, I know, I know. That one party scarred you for life and the subject is off the table forever. For the record, you slept alone last night. I was on the couch in case you needed me, but I'll sleep in the bed in my office if you decide to stay."

That was the answer he'd been waiting for. Ken had slept on the couch. They hadn't given in to desire and ripped each other's clothes off. Why was Brady disappointed?

"Here's the plan, Finn. You're going to take a shower and think about what you want to do. Stay with me and help someone that no one else can, or go home and deal with your family's expectations. Either way, your duffel is at the foot of the bed and there's a clean towel and packaged toothbrush for you in the bathroom."

Ken released him and took a step back. "I'll have breakfast waiting when you're done and we can talk about what you've decided."

Brady let the dictatorial tone slide as he thought

about his options. Home or Tanaka. Judgmental concern or dangerous temptation. He could always take door number three, he knew. Just leave. Go somewhere with the money he'd inherited from his mother and start again. Alone.

Shower. Right now he just wanted a shower. "I appreciate it. This. All the trouble you're going to."

Ken turned away and his long black braid swung with the motion, striking Brady's side. "Don't thank me again, Finn. Just say yes."

He wanted to. He studied Tanaka's tattooed back with hungry eyes and wanted to agree to anything he asked. The strength of his desire scared him. It had from the moment they met.

Without his self-control he'd have nothing. That was why, if he were a smart man, he would say no to the job and get the hell out of there. Being around Ken Tanaka made him unpredictable. Tempted him to let go and give in.

He swore under his breath and headed toward the shower. Last night proved he wasn't that bright. One evening of drinking was all it had taken to alienate family, nearly embarrass them all online and go home with the one man he most wanted to avoid.

He was never drinking again.

CHAPTER TWO

"Tanaka?" Brady walked out of the bedroom buttoning his jeans, his black shirt thrown over his shoulder. "Am I dreaming, or do I smell bacon?"

He was starving. Whatever was in that nasty swamp remedy, it had done the trick. If he hadn't watched the video with his own eyes, Brady could almost convince himself he'd never gotten drunk at all.

He saw a covered plate with a Post-it note beside it. *Taking an office call then grabbing a shower for myself. Eat.*

"You don't have to tell me twice." Brady saw the carafe of orange juice and poured some in a large glass with ice before carrying it and his plate to the living room. He'd been here before, though he'd spent most of

27

his time across the hall in Tanaka's office—basically a studio apartment filled with computer towers, monitors and the kind of surveillance equipment that would make any super spy envious.

Ken didn't just own a downtown loft in a refurbished three-story warehouse—he owned and lived in the entire building. The first time Brady followed him here and saw his living space, he'd wondered aloud if the Scottish-Japanese technophile wanted to be Batman.

"You already have the lair, the finances and the right equipment," he'd said.

"Why do you ask? Do you have a fetish for rich men in masks?" Ken asked, smiling that angelic smile.

"I don't have fetishes," Brady responded quickly. "But he isn't my type. He's got a cave full of baggage and relies on toys instead of natural talent. Give me Superman any day."

Tanaka's expression had changed, a flash of irritation mixed with hunger. "He's got plenty of natural talent," he'd muttered before changing the conversation back to the Finn family's Burke problem.

Sitting on the leather couch, Brady set his glass on the coffee table and dug into his vegetable omelet and crisp bacon while studying the loft with fresh eyes. It was big enough to fit a car inside and still have room for a party. So much open space for one man, though the way it was laid out created the feel of several rooms without the use of hallways or closed doors.

The man who hacked into other people's private lives obviously didn't feel the need for his own privacy—either that or his decorator was one of those Peeping Toms from the club. There wasn't even a door to his bathroom, just frosted glass blocks forming a partition between it and the living room.

That had given Brady pause...until he'd experienced the shower itself. It seemed to be made with his six-foot-five height and wide frame in mind. A rain showerhead sprouted from the ceiling, rather than the wall-mounted type that usually hit him squarely in the chest, and there was plenty of room to turn around. By the time he'd finished, he was considering staying and doing the job for the shower alone.

And that bed... Brady was not a small man, but he'd only taken up half the space on a mattress that was exactly firm enough and covered with sheets that felt like fluffy damn clouds. The mattress and the frame had to be custom made, since for the first time in his life his feet didn't hang off the end. Call him Goldilocks, but that bed was just right.

He could only imagine what Ken needed with a bed like that. Orgies came to mind. Kinky, BDSM free-for-alls with plenty of lube and restraints to go around. His cock twitched at the thought of Ken and lube, and Brady frowned down at his empty plate, wishing he hadn't eaten so fast. The food had been delicious and eating would distract him from thinking about sex.

Why did Tanaka have to be so damn perfect at everything? Cool computer genius, athletic martial artist, super sleuth, master chef and—according to Tasha and Owen—king of all things rope related. But those two had no idea where his true talents lay.

Brady exhaled and set down his plate so he could adjust himself through the snug denim as he thought about Ken's wickedly skilled mouth. He'd had his first taste of that skill at Burke's. They'd caught each other in the act, both snooping around somewhere they didn't belong. Brady had set out to test Tanaka, to make sure he wouldn't run to Burke to tell him the senator's body man was in his private office. Faster than he'd expected, the casual interrogation had become intimate and laced with sexual innuendo. Before he knew it he was leaning against the desk and Ken was devastating him with his mouth, undoing his pants and leaving Brady too stunned to respond.

It still shocked him when he thought about it. How he'd been drawn to him like a magnet to metal from minute one. Tasha interrupted them just in time and he had to be grateful. One more taste of those talented lips and taunting tongue and Brady would have had Ken Tanaka right there on the floor, without knowing or caring that they were both on the same side. Both working for the feds to trip up their host.

He'd tried to steer clear after that, shaken by his own behavior, and then everything had gone to hell. Tasha ran away and Stephen lost it, and all Brady wanted to do, all he could think about doing for weeks, was fixing it. Luckily, Ken had the same idea.

A few months later the two men were being hailed as conquering heroes at the reunited couple's wedding reception. Brady hadn't wanted the attention but Ken had loved it, spending the evening pressing up against Brady each time someone wanted a picture. When the photographer asked for a shot of Ken and Brady with the bride and groom on the dock, Brady had seen Ken whispering in the grinning Tasha's ear. A few minutes later all three men were in the lake and Tasha had gotten her favorite snapshot of the wedding. She'd actually had it framed and placed on her fireplace mantle.

It was right after that—when Ken followed Brady into his room for a change of clothes—that things had gotten personal again, just as quickly as it had happened before. One minute they were laughing and tugging at their wet jackets, the next Brady was shoving his soaked shirt in his mouth to mute his passionate shouts as Ken knelt in front of him and swallowed his cock.

Brady groaned and the sound echoed through the open loft. Thinking about the things Ken had done with his tongue, with the muscles in his throat, brought Brady instantly to the edge.

He was in a bad way. Maybe it was time to take a page out of his younger brother Rory's playbook. Rory Finn never went to bed wanting. When he was on duty, he was the best EMT in the city, focused and indefatigable. He took his extracurricular activities just as seriously. If he saw a man he wanted—old, young, doctor, lawyer, waiter—he was relentless. Fearless.

For Brady, sex needed to mean something. Even before he'd enlisted and hook-ups got more complicated, he'd never been big on one-night stands. He'd always wanted more. But he hadn't been with anyone in over a year—not since his ex went career instead of accepting his discharge. Marine-for-life meant no building a life together. In hindsight, that surprisingly unemotional break-up had been the right call, making his decision to come home a few months later a hell of a lot simpler. But it didn't help him with his current predicament. At this point if he didn't get over himself and find someone to sleep with soon, he would lose his fucking mind.

There's someone right across the hall.

Unable to resist, Brady reached for the oddly-shaped remote on the coffee table and pushed a button, opening the floor-to-ceiling cabinet to reveal multiple monitors. One was tuned into a local news channel, but the rest were for personal security.

Ken had pointed this out the last time he was here. "You called me Batman?" he'd laughed. "Here's another toy."

Tanaka had cameras installed in his office, the gym that took up the entire second floor and an atrium that took up the first—a green, peaceful paradise complete with a hammock and a koi pond guarding the service elevator. Brady shook his head. He should have gone into computers instead of the family business—a career in freelance hacking was clearly more lucrative.

Brady focused on Ken's office chair. That was where he *should* be, but the chair was empty. He rotated the small toggle that looked like it belonged on a videogame controller and watched the image change as the camera panned to find its target. It passed a line of laptops and flat-screened monitors and a small kitchenette that was cluttered with computer parts. When it had gone as far as it could, it was pointing directly at a clear glass wall dripping with water from another overhead shower.

"*Jesus.*"

What the hell did the man have against solid walls and doors?

Ken was facing the camera, and the glass did nothing to hinder the view. Brady shuddered. Heaven help him, but the view was too beautiful to resist. Ken stretched like a cat as the water flow over every lean, coiling muscle in his body. He tilted his head, his long braid wrapped in a masculine bun that made his neck seem more vulnerable. Brady wanted to scrape his teeth along that flesh. To mark it.

Ken's hand slid down his smooth, hairless body to the hard cock between his legs, and Brady couldn't resist unbuttoning his own jeans to join him.

He shouldn't. He shouldn't be doing this at all—

watching. Invading someone's privacy. He wasn't some pervert who got his kicks peeping in windows. Hell, he didn't even watch porn or go to strip clubs. He never got the point of purposely paying to watch and want something he'd never be allowed to touch. But when it came to this man, he couldn't look away.

Did Ken know his camera could point in that direction? Did he know Brady was watching him stroke himself in graceful, fluid motions as if performing for his lover? As if he had all the time in the world?

"Too slow," Brady whispered. "Don't tease me."

His own fingers were clumsy and rough on his thick, sensitive shaft. He pulled it out and gripped it firmly in his fist. He wanted to be in that shower. Wanted to be standing behind Ken, or sitting on the bench against the wall and lowering that body onto his cock. Wanted to drive him wild until he was begging Brady to come. "Beg me, Tanaka."

Ken arched his back as if he'd heard him, his fist shuttling faster up and down his length.

"That's right. Fuck, that's perfect." Brady matched his rhythm, his eyes unblinking as he memorized every detail of the scene. He swore and shook his head when Ken's movements slowed, but then he realized the man on the screen was reaching for a bottle of clear liquid. Lube?

Ken coated his fingers and reached around behind him, his lips parting on a mute gasp. *Yes.*

"You kinky fucking bastard. What are you up to?"

But Brady knew what was happening. Ken was pushing his fingers into his own ass, stretching it, craving something Brady wanted to give him. If they'd given in to each other last night, he could walk over there right now and take it. Lose himself. Lose control.

It's tight isn't it? That's right, lean against the glass so you can go deeper. Get it ready for me. Get that ass ready.

Ken's forehead and free hand were pressed against the wet glass as he rocked back into his fingers. Brady licked his lips and flicked his thumb over the tip of his shaft, shuddering. "Damn, I wish you would turn around and do that."

Once again, as if responding to his demands, Ken slipped his fingers out and turned his back to the camera. Brady was so enthralled by his bitable cheeks he didn't notice what was stuck to the bench until Ken approached it and drenched it with lube. He'd never been jealous of a dildo before, but when Ken got in position and lowered his ass onto it, when he closed his eyes and an expression of pure ecstasy transformed his face, Brady gritted his teeth and nearly bruised his cock with his white-knuckled grip.

That's mine.

His thoughts were primitive. Aggressive. They didn't make sense. He'd turned Ken away more than once and vowed never to give in to his desires. But that didn't stop him from wanting to claim him. In some dark, hidden place in his mind, he already had.

When Ken held onto the bench with one hand, his erection with the other, and started to move, Brady lifted his hips off the couch, imagining his was the cock being ridden. "Oh yeah. Oh, that's good. Give me that ass, Tanaka. Ride *me*."

He couldn't stop the commands from escaping his lips. It was his fantasy, and in it, he wanted Tanaka to hear him. Wanted him to do as he said. Brady was so turned on he could hardly breathe, but it wasn't enough. Not for this need inside him. A need Ken had put there with his casual comments this morning.

"You want more than a quick ride too, don't you? You want *me*. What if I gave you your damn noncon?" he growled at the monitor. "What if I ripped you off that fake dick and forced you to take every inch of me instead?"

He could see it playing out in his head in graphic detail. The camera catching everything as he surprised Ken in the shower. The shock, the struggle to get him to the floor with one arm pinned behind his back and his ass in the air like an offering.

This was no gentle daydream. Nothing he would admit to without shame. It was animalistic and vulgar and hot as hell. And because it wasn't real he didn't go slow. Didn't take the time for his lover to adjust. He was too far gone for that. Ken *had* been begging for it, and Brady would make him take it. Love it.

"That's what you said, isn't it? Make you love it when I fuck you into the floor until you can't move. When I pound your ass until you scream. You want it. Look at how greedy you are. You want me fucking you so hard. *Fuck…*"

Brady watched Ken's strong body pump up and down on the dildo as his hand stroked his cock. He was close. Brady was too, his body on fire, but he wanted them to come together. Needed it in a way he couldn't explain.

He saw Ken's mouth open on a silent shout and then

he was with him. Lightning sparred with the live wires sizzling along his spine and his body stiffened. Jets of hot semen spurted on his stomach and chest and he heard himself mumbling Ken's name with each shuddering wave of his release.

It took him a minute or two to get his breathing back under control. To remember where he was. When he did, all he could do was marvel at how hard he'd come. He couldn't remember the last time he'd had an orgasm that intense. He'd never imagined he could get so turned on from that kind of twisted, dark... Jesus, there was something seriously wrong with him.

Brady stood and wove dizzily from the head rush, making his way to the bathroom with his hand still shaking on his shaft. He rinsed himself off in the sink, trembling as he splashed cold water on the back of his neck.

He could barely look at himself in the mirror. The things he'd thought, the things he'd said *out loud*. Orders he couldn't believe he'd given. He'd gotten off on the idea of taking Ken without permission. Without holding back.

Brady didn't indulge in aggressive passion or rough sex. His size made it impossible to consider. He was a brute. A clumsy ox. He'd started sprouting up at ten-years-old and he'd learned early on to be mindful of his strength, particularly in physical situations. Fighting and then, as he got older, sex.

His ex had been a rough-and-tumble leatherneck with muscle to spare and Brady had still never been able to truly let go with him. Brady wasn't passionate enough, the angry Marine would tell him. He didn't want it enough.

It was an argument Brady couldn't win and he knew it...until he'd met Tanaka.

What just happened was passionate enough and he'd wanted it too much to resist. It had been intense and out of control, and it had only been a fantasy.

That shouldn't happen in the real world. If he did this job, if he stayed, he had to resist this thing between them. He didn't trust himself not to lose control around Ken and, despite Tanaka's strength, he didn't want to risk hurting him.

He dried off, pulled his shirt over his head and re-buttoned his jeans, thinking about that dildo. He hadn't expected that. He'd thought Ken was exclusively a top. That because of his lifestyle he would have to be in charge in every way.

Did Doms even give blowjobs?

He obviously didn't know shit about that bondage-sado-whatever the hell it was. All he knew was that the few times things between them had gotten heated, Ken had been the one pleasuring him. And Brady had loved it.

Stop thinking about his mouth. Brady turned off the monitors and closed the cabinet, grabbing his plate on the way back to the kitchen. He rinsed it off and was setting it on the drying rack when he saw his phone on the counter. The message light was pulsing.

It looked like it had been ringing all morning. He decided to listen to his calls as he cleaned the rest of the dishes. It was the least he could do to curb his guilt after breakfast and that shower.

He dialed his voicemail and turned on the speaker, smiling a little when he heard Owen's voice.

New message. Today at nine a.m.

"Good morning. I have a headache and I have a feeling you do too. I just wanted to call and tell you about the long-winded, *very public* advice some drunk gave me last night at the pub. It's a funny story. I'm already planning his payback. By the way, you're going to get kicked out of Finn Club unless you can follow the rules. The first rule of Finn Club? You're Irish, learn how to drink. Call me when you get this."

New message. Today at nine-thirty-five a.m.

"Brady, it's Owen again. I actually wanted to talk to you about what you said last night. In case you're wondering? I'm not mad. In fact, you lit a fire under my ass and I love you for it. This morning I've been looking into your suggestion and I think I've found the answer, but I need to run it by our resident Cupid. Call me so I know you survived the Great Rumming of 2015. Oh and the second rule of Finn club is that tall is good, but too tall is just showing off. Cut it out."

New message. Today at nine-fifty-one a.m.

"Hey Brady, Seamus here. Owen said you aren't answering your phone. Call and I promise not to give you my lecture about sneaking behind the bar for another bottle after the bartender has cut you off. Oh, and my brother wants me to tell you that the third rule is not to talk about Finn Club, whatever that means. Help me out and call him please, he's driving me crazy and I have to help Penny and Wes with their art projects."

Brady laughed and shook his head, scrubbing the omelet pan.

New message. Today at ten-fifteen a.m.

"Owen again. Are you tied up right now? You went home with Tanaka so this is a legitimate question. If you are, use your safe word and when you can feel your dialing fingers, call me back. I mean it. I just bought plane tickets instead of pizza and you aren't around to stop me. Who knows what I'll do next?"

New message. Today at ten-forty-eight a.m.

"I'm officially worried. Call me in the next two hours or I'm dialing 911. Your brothers basically own that number, so the odds of them being the ones to catch you naked, hogtied and covered in peanut butter are pretty damn good. This is your last warning."

Brady dried his hands and reached for the phone to text Owen, but there was one more message that had come almost immediately after Owen's last call. He hoped his cousin hadn't called Solomon. The last thing he needed was his older brother finding out about his drunken bar rant.

"This message is for Brady Finn from Calvin Grimes. I received an interesting email alert this morning. I'm not sure who sent it, but the subject heading was your name and the link attached led to a video of you in your family's pub. Your speech was...stirring. And what you said made me think you might finally be ready to go on

43

that date with me. Who wants to live like a monk, right? How about we start tonight with a drink at Tango's and see what happens? No pressure. I'll be waiting for your call."

"What the fuck?" Brady frowned. He was sure he'd rejected Stephen's persistent yes-man enough times that he'd gotten the message. How had he, of all people, gotten his hands on that link?

"That was me."

Ken's voice made him drop his phone in the sink. Brady swore and picked it up again, drying it off on his jeans. "Shit, sorry, I didn't hear you come in. What was you?"

Ken's expression was not as relaxed as it should have been for a man who'd just starred in the hottest shower scene Brady had ever witnessed. "Lover boy's call? I did that. I sent him the link before shutting the video down. I figured he'd see it as a sign and call you."

It was hard to concentrate when all he could see was an image of Ken's face mid-orgasm. He'd sent Cal the link on purpose? "You *wanted* him to ask me out?"

Ken moved closer. "And I want you to call him back and say yes."

Brady knew he looked as confused as he felt. "No

way in hell."

Ken's smile was subtle, the relaxing of his shoulders barely visible, but Brady noticed. He liked his answer. "I'm not happy about it either, but this is the job, Finn. Calvin Grimes is the job. At least, your part of it. He's my way in, and the only way I have to get to him is through you."

"Hell." Brady looked at his phone and sighed. How had he found out about Cal's crush? Had he hacked the suggestive email messages Grimes had sent him during his time working for the senator, or had Tasha spilled the beans? "Did you tell me this last night? Because I can't see me getting drunk enough to think this was a good idea. Cal Grimes isn't quite right, Tanaka. He's like a terrier. If he bites down it could be hard to shake him off."

"I might have skipped the finer points. You were drunk, remember? But don't worry. I want you to meet him but I'm not planning on leaving you alone with him. Not for a minute."

Brady raised one eyebrow. "He might not appreciate the extra company. He's very…focused." Disturbingly fixated was more accurate.

"He'll never know I'm there. But you will."

That sounded intriguing. "I think I'm recovered enough for you to fill me in now. Why is Grimes my part of the job? Who are you trying to get to? Should we call in Stephen? Are we after a senator?"

"So you're staying?"

Brady sighed, knowing it was never a question. "For the moment. With Cal involved, I make no promises."

"Then we'll start planning after you call Owen. I think that would be—what—the fourth rule of Finn Club?"

He'd been listening at the door. Sneaky *and* kinky. But then, after today Brady didn't have room to talk. "Smartass."

He made the call.

Chapter Three

He should be getting hazard pay or compensation for mental pain and suffering. Ken was going to owe him one for this. A big one.

When his date left their small table to find the harried waiter and order another round, Brady took advantage of the breather, rubbing his temples in an effort to both ease his tension headache and erase the images Calvin Grimes had been trying to tempt him with for the last hour.

To his credit, Cal had managed ten solid minutes of harmless small talk before he started making propositions. He told him about a timeshare he had in the Bahamas. Beautiful beaches, great weather…and wouldn't Brady like to join him for a private weekend? No pressure. Brady had turned him down gently, reminding him of his red hair and his family's tendency to boil like lobsters in the sun.

Cal was gracious, moving on to a molecular gastronomy event he'd been invited to in Washington. He wanted to take Brady so they could drink coffee *air* while eating *deconstructed* meatloaf with well-connected socialites. They'd have to share a suite at the hotel, of course, but Brady would have his own bed if he chose to use it. With as much calm as he could muster, Brady declined, lying about a sensitive stomach and busy schedule.

Cal's determination to get in his pants was unsettling. It made him feel like a piece of meat, or the last task in a high stakes scavenger hunt.

Grimes was everything he'd seemed. A climber. A big talker and a status junkie. He'd been Stephen's assistant, but in between his not-remotely-subtle advances, Brady learned he'd recently branched out into consulting. Opposition research for select political clients who were desperate for ammunition against their competitors.

It was a sleazy job but, according to Cal, it paid well. He'd made sure Brady knew *how* well at least twice in the conversation. But despite his attempts to impress, so far all his invitations were having the opposite effect. He should have done more research before the date.

Brady reminded himself why he was doing this. Ken hadn't told him everything, but it had been enough. Some poor sucker had gotten caught up in a bad relationship with an influential man and fallen off the grid. It was Ken's job to find him, and he admitted that he'd expected it to be easy. He'd been wrong. He was still looking six months later.

Freelancing for the feds on the Burke case had been his chance to scan the blackmailer's private files. Ken knew Burke kept dossiers on powerful men and their weaknesses and he was hoping to find more information on a particular investor he considered his prime suspect. He'd found more than he'd bargained for.

It had taken a few months for Ken to sift through the data that connected his suspect to a group of powerful, practically untouchable men. Burke's notes on them contained their questionable habits, some cryptic words and phrases he couldn't understand, and a record of the few sloppy hotel room incidents with escorts Burke had managed to sweep under the rug in return for favors and insider information. Most of the men in this group were nicknamed according to their perversion, but one or two real names had been written down. Sadly, the names didn't lead to anything helpful. Each one was so good at covering their tracks that Ken, with all his talent, hadn't been able to hack them yet. From their firewalls and snares, he believed there had to be guys like him on the payroll to make sure of it.

But Ken didn't give up. He'd been using a new program to find another way in when luck led him to one loose link in the chain. It was a fairly recent outside connection that wasn't in Burke's notes and no one had taken the time to conceal—Calvin Grimes.

Apparently Cal didn't just offer his services to senators. Brady wasn't sure what he did for *these* men, but Ken said it didn't matter. Their job consisted of finding and retrieving a single man, not taking down a Cabal. Dating Cal was a fishing expedition. And Brady was the only bait for the job.

"Finn, I can hear you frowning. You're on a date. It's a bad date, I admit it, but I never promised you a love match. You have to give him something to work with. Pretend to find him interesting."

Brady grimaced. *Think of the devil and he talks in your ear.*

Ken wasn't helping the situation at all. He'd been

listening in on every moment of this travesty, distracting Brady with his sultry voice and provocative comments. It made him wish he could see him, wish that Ken was the one across the table.

"We can switch places," Brady offered. "You two have more in common anyway. You like nice things, money, fancy food—"

"Giant sexy gingers with repressed but explosive sexual energy just begging to be tapped," Ken interrupted smoothly.

"No one's doing any tapping."

"Not for lack of trying. He's practically bending over with a Ride Me sign on his ass and he hasn't even seen you naked. I suppose we have to be thankful for small favors. If he knew what those jeans of yours were working overtime to conceal, he'd be useless."

Brady was glad Ken couldn't see his face. He hated blushing. "*You* know and you seem to be doing fine."

"I have better self-control. It comes from the years of training you don't like me to talk about. Believe me, if I didn't have it, I'd be the one bending over that table and begging."

Brady huffed out a nervous laugh, sliding forward to hide his erection from the crowded bar. "I can't see you begging, *Master* Tanaka."

Not outside of my fantasies

"The night is young. Wait until we get home."

Cal appeared beside the table, water and one martini in his hands. "You look flushed, Brady. Is it too crowded in here?"

"No." Brady took the water and drank it gratefully. Ken's words had turned up the heat and made it difficult to concentrate. "I needed this. I must still be a little hung over. I don't think I'll be drinking again anytime soon."

"That's not why you're blushing." Ken sounded smug.

Cal sat down and smiled, reaching out to cover Brady's hand where it lay on the table. Brady fought against his instincts and kept it there. "I understand. I should have waited to take you out, but once I get an idea in my head I'm like a dog with a bone."

Ken snorted. "Or a terrier with a boner."

"Stop," Brady demanded. Realizing Cal thought he was talking to him, he hurried to add, "I mean, there's no need to apologize. Though I *was* surprised when you called."

"Why?"

"Well, I wasn't that fun to be around at the office,

and you have to admit we don't have much in common."

"Good recovery."

Cal's smile widened and Brady could practically see the wheels turning and the calculation in his eyes. "I get it. I think I understand what's been off between us."

That I don't like you?

"You're right. In many ways we're different people. Opposites." Cal sent him an endearing smile, his brown hair swooping down to cover one brown eye in a way that reminded Brady his date wasn't unattractive. "You're a veteran of the police force and our country's military. You don't have to make deals or soothe ruffled feathers. You don't have to impress anyone and you probably don't understand why other people do. People who have to make their living at it, like I do."

Ken chuckled. "He's aiming for humble and insightful now. A true sign of desperation."

"I'm not planning on staying in that position long, mind you, but my career goals aren't the issue here. The issue is we're both just people who want something more than we have. Someone who could belong to us." Cal sent him a look of admiration. "What you said in that video really spoke to me, Brady. Your cousin Owen *should* appreciate what he has."

"Oh he does," Brady assured him. "He's been going through a rough patch with the transition, that's all. It's understandable."

Cal shrugged. "I suppose. I've been out of the closet since before I got my first paper route so I have to admit, when Stephen told me about his straight brother finding love and playing house with a talented man like Jeremy Porter, I was dubious. I mean just imagining that alpha male construction worker, who never met a woman he couldn't bang, deciding to experiment on a whim…" Cal shook his head, bemused. "It doesn't seem fair that he made zero effort and still got to take home the grand prize."

"Oh hell," Ken groaned through the earpiece. "You're going to hit him, aren't you?"

Brady frowned dangerously, his need to defend his cousin making him forget himself, but Cal quickly backtracked. "I'm sorry, I spoke without thinking. And I'm not saying I'm not happy for two people in love. I am. But I'm human too and humans are inherently selfish creatures. I was thinking about me. Thinking about wanting what Owen and Jeremy have, just like you do."

Once he'd forced down his cutting response and

taken a calming breath, Brady didn't have to lie. "I wouldn't mind knowing what that felt like. Last night I—I shouldn't have said anything to Owen. I wouldn't have if I wasn't drunk, because I've lived with those two and seen how good they are together day in and day out. What they have is pretty damn rare."

And it had been decades in the making. Owen and Jeremy had been best friends since their school days and knew each other better than anyone else ever could. When they'd added sex and romance to the mix, it just made it that much sweeter.

Brady didn't know anyone that well. He and his brothers had been raised more like a sports team or a military unit, with a firm hand and a short leash. Brady never had the opportunity to form relationships, outside of family, that he could trust. Not until he enlisted, and by then he was set in his ways. He would die for any of the men he fought beside, but he hesitated when it came to giving his heart.

And now? After all the things he'd seen and done, he just wasn't sure that kind of love was ever going to be in the cards for him. But he couldn't pretend he didn't want it to be.

"My parents love each other like that," Cal offered,

looking nervous and desperate to get out of what he'd stepped in. "They've been in love since middle school. Never had a moment's doubt that they were meant for each other, or that their child would be the first gay president. They wanted me to make my mark on the world. Unfortunately I shattered that last dream when I told them I'd never campaign for an eight-year temp job as a human piñata. There are other ways to power, and those ways include large amounts of cash and less bad press."

Brady relaxed at the change to a safer, less sexually objectifying and insulting subject. "It's always nice to hear about two people sticking it out that long. Stephen's parents are the same. Ellen said she knew the minute he took her hand that he was the one. They've been together close to forty years and they still act like lovesick teenagers."

"Yes, I know, Stephen Finn has the perfect family bio for political campaigns." Cal narrowed his brown eyes on Brady. "His parents...but not yours?"

Brady tensed and sent him a look of disbelief. "I think you already know the answer to that, Mr. Oppo Research."

Cal looked uncomfortable. "You're a Finn and the

senator's cousin, of course I know. I just didn't want you to think I investigate my dates as a rule. Besides, I'd rather hear your take on it."

"So would I," Ken murmured close to his mic. "But you don't share your secrets unless you're rum-drunk."

Brady slid his hand away from Cal's and took another drink of water. "My take isn't that much different from what's on paper."

"I doubt that. Your father raising six boys on his own while working as the Chief of police? It sounds like you'd have a lot of stories."

Brady sent Cal a look that made him squirm. "Solomon the Elder had a knack for keeping men in line. He wasn't that good at keeping women happy. Nobody's perfect."

Three wives had proven that, though no one could say he hadn't done the right thing by them. Six months after Uncle Shawn married Ellen, Sol had found himself the groom in a genuine shotgun wedding, complete with a pregnant, crying bride and angry father-in-law. Donna had given birth to Solomon Jr. and James, and then she had second thoughts about her husband. She'd tried to take the boys when she left but Sol wouldn't stand for it. The Finn name was his to protect after his father and grandfather had done their best to ruin it. The boys were Finns and they would grow up knowing the value of that name. That was all that mattered.

Not too long after that, a statuesque pageant winner with auburn hair and perfect pedigree had gotten to ride in a parade car with the divorced but still dashing officer. When Rose became pregnant, her parents threatened to disown her if she married Sol, which of course had sent her straight into his arms. She'd been young and sweet and in no way ready to become an instant housewife to a distant man or the mother of three wild toddlers. Sol had had a meeting with her parents and their lawyer and come to an arrangement.

"Your mother... She signed away her visitation rights and moved to Paris, right? That must have been hard."

Wishing Cal would start talking about his timeshare again, Brady sent him a look of warning. "Not on me. I was too young to remember."

"Brady." Ken's voice was like a tender kiss. "Are you okay?"

It was an old ache, knowing she'd let her parents agree to give Sol full custody in exchange for a quickie divorce. But his mother hadn't disappeared from his life entirely. When Brady was old enough, she'd started writing to him once a week, posing as a pen pal so Sol wouldn't forbid the communication. Each letter had been warm and loving and full of all the laughter his regimented house was lacking. He'd lived for those letters. A few years ago, after she died, he'd found out she'd left him not only the healthy inheritance he'd been living off of since he got out of the service, but also her home in Paris. He'd never been to see it, and he hadn't told Sol about it either. The old man hadn't even let her send Christmas presents, so Brady could only imagine how he would react if he knew about the house. It wasn't something he was ready to face.

"The third wife lasted longer, though." Was Cal trying to lighten the mood? Why wouldn't he let this go? "The last three boys are all hers, right? And they might have stayed together if she hadn't..."

Wyatt and Noah's mom had died from complications while giving birth to Rory. But she wouldn't have lasted either. Laney had handed Sol divorce papers a few hours before she went into labor. Brady was six at the time, but he still remembered the shouting match they'd had that day.

"I'm not her. Stop comparing me to her!"

He looked at Cal's wide eyes and shook his head

ruefully. "Look, this is a little personal, Calvin. I know I didn't give you much choice since I suck at small talk. I'm sorry. Maybe this wasn't such a good idea."

"Don't be sorry, please. I was the one prying. I'm eager to know everything there is to know about you." Cal definitely sounded eager. "My work is full of small talk, socially acceptable topics and twisted truths. I want all the messy details on Brady Finn. Like, why would you decide to stay at your cousin's house instead of going back to your family home? Why haven't you gone back to your old job on the force? What happened to you overseas that seems to make you so sad when you think no one's looking? I *have* to know the real you."

He already seemed to know one hell of a lot.

It's a job, Brady. Focus on the job and tighten up. He left you an opening.

He forced a flattered smile. "Well, the real me sounds like a winner, doesn't he? Maybe someone you could grab a drink with, I suppose. Or a little something on the side at a timeshare? But you just proved my point, Cal. No matter how much we might like it to be otherwise, there's no way I'd fit in your life or the circles you travel in. No way your impressive friends would think I was good enough."

"Perfect, Finn," Ken crooned. "And you said you wouldn't be good at this."

The expression that crossed Cal's face was surprising in its intensity. "You'll fit because I want you to. And I think I've made it pretty clear that *you are* what I want. I knew it the first time I saw you."

"You did?" He wasn't sure how else to respond.

"I did. I won't lie to you. I think it's obvious what's been on my mind all night. Not taking you out to my car and getting in your pants has been a true show of willpower on my part."

"And intelligence," Ken muttered to no one in particular.

"I'm not…ready for that," Brady offered, looking down as if he were uncomfortable. Which he was. "I need to get to know a man a little better before I go there."

Cal narrowed his eyes. "That's why we're here. Look at that blush. I didn't know a big Marine like you would blush like that. Do you *not* know how many men are watching you right now, undressing you with their eyes? I'm the envy of all of them. It would be that way everywhere we went. Especially those social circles you're worried about. They wouldn't care what you said or how you dressed; one look and all they'd be able to think about was getting you naked and what they could do to you when you were. But they wouldn't dare try. Not if you were mine."

Brady was definitely turning red now, though he was more insulted and embarrassed than flattered. Cal was more aggressive than he'd imagined. He made himself shrug it off, wondering how much longer this had to go on. "I'm pretty sure that's not what they'd be thinking."

"No?"

He forced a self-conscious laugh. "I'm a big guy with bright red hair. I've got two left feet and I don't like crowds. I stick out like a sore thumb."

Cal licked his lips. "You are definitely big, but believe me, that's not a drawback. I want you on my arm. Want to show you off. I honestly can't believe no one has chained you to their bed yet. That you're available. *Were* available," he corrected with a sly smile.

"Wow. That's really…nice. I mean, that you want to go out again." Ken couldn't say he wasn't trying to be polite. All Brady had to do now was *not* grab the back of Cal's head and slam it into the table. If he could keep that instinct in check, they'd be fine.

"We'll be going out again, Brady," Cal assured him.

"But the night's not over yet. Let's see where it takes us."

Ken swore in Brady's earpiece, making him flinch. "Excuse yourself and go to the restrooms. Now."

Brady stood abruptly, unable to resist that tone of command. "I'm—I'll be back in a minute."

Cal's smile was cocky and determined. "You look flushed again. I'll get you more water."

Men were definitely sizing him up as he pushed his way through the crowd at Tango's. Maybe they thought he looked familiar. Most of them had probably dated his brother. Rory had once told Brady he came to Tango's when he wasn't in the mood for a challenge.

Brady sighed. Rory was going to get himself in trouble one day with his preference for straight men. If there were four men in a room and three of them were handsome, available and gay, Rory would focus on the angst-ridden heterosexual with girl troubles every time. He'd get him too. At least long enough to prove to himself that he could.

His baby brother had been the only one who wasn't surprised when Owen moved in with Jeremy. "Owen was never satisfied, no matter how many women he went through. And he spent all his free time at Jeremy's house. There were a million clues."

"I didn't see it." His brother James had shaken his head. "Honestly, I thought he might have had a sex addiction, like the guy on that cable show. Seamus thought the same thing."

"I didn't care yesterday and I don't care today." Solomon frowned at his younger brothers. "He's family and he's happy. Move on."

Wyatt shrugged. "You may not care, but I'm fascinated. I thought the Quarterback was one hundred percent straight. Jeremy must be truly talented."

"No man is one hundred percent straight," Rory informed his brothers. "That's a fact."

"That's *your* dream, Rory," Noah had laughed. "Stop projecting."

"That's my reality. I'm just waiting for everyone else to catch up."

Pushing open the bathroom door, Brady shared a quick, awkward glance with a bearded hipster in a bow tie washing his hands. Then he looked at himself in the mirror. He could use a little of Rory's confidence about now. This was the first job he'd ever had that was all about being attractive—in this case specifically to Cal Grimes. It was disconcerting, and it made him think about himself in an entirely new and uncomfortable way.

He genuinely didn't get Cal's interest—well, except for the physical desire, but he was working a lot harder than he had to if sex was all he wanted. Cal wasn't bad to look at and he had a good job. Half the bar would probably be up for a quickie in the parking lot if he asked them.

But he'd set his sights on Brady, who didn't mingle, didn't enjoy talking politics, and who'd rather grab a cheeseburger and watch a baseball game than dress up to eat a plate of nothing that cost more than his monthly bills. What was it the lusty Cal saw that he liked?

Whatever it is, Ken sees it too.

Brady took a closer look. He had blues eyes, the same as pretty much everyone in his family. He'd gotten the auburn hair from his mother, a strong jawline from Sol, and his maternal grandfather had given him his oversized build. He had a harder look than his younger brothers, but when he laughed he sounded just like Noah.

It was strange, but that was always how he'd seen himself—as pieces of other people. A Finn. One of Sol's boys. A Marine. But now he was trying to see himself without them. To see himself through another man's eyes. Just Brady. He still didn't think he was handsome in the ordinary sense, but he supposed he wasn't bad for bait. His reflection sent him a rueful grin.

Anyway, he supposed as long as Cal liked his looks and got him in front of the people they were looking for before spiking his drink and dragging him to bed, he was doing the job Ken needed.

He'd much rather be doing something else. Someone else. He tapped his tiny earpiece impatiently when bowtie guy walked back out into the bar. Why had Ken sent him to the bathroom?

A stall opened and Brady swore in surprise when Ken dragged him in and closed and locked the door behind him. "*What the fuck?* I thought you were listening from the coffee shop across the street."

"Don't talk," Ken ordered in a harsh whisper. "We won't be alone for long and I need to make sure you're okay."

"I'm ok—" Talented lips stole his breath, opening his mouth so Ken's tongue could tangle with Brady's. *God, yes. Too long.* How had he stayed away so long?

He leaned back against the door when he felt his knees weaken, and Ken followed, his fingers digging into Brady's scalp and pulling his head down for more.

More. He would never get enough of Ken's mouth. He wanted it on him everywhere. His hands curved around the cheeks of Ken's firm ass and squeezed, dragging him closer.

More.

Ken lifted his mouth enough to bite down sharply on Brady's lower lip. A rumbling growl escaped his throat and Ken smiled. "There he is. There's my beast. That little weasel doesn't get to touch you."

"Never," Brady growled again.

Ken's hand pressed between their bodies and Brady felt him undoing the buttons of his jeans. "Tanaka…"

"Finn," Ken echoed teasingly. "Just a taste, that's all. To keep you on your toes and clear all that flattery out of your head."

Strong, graceful fingers wrapped around his hard shaft and he moaned raggedly. "Here? In the fucking men's room of a gay bar?"

Ken snorted. "Don't tell me you've never done this before. Never met a sexy stranger in a bar and ended up just like this, getting hard on the idea that someone could walk in and hear your greedy moans."

"Never," Brady moaned.

Ken's gaze narrowed in surprise, his fingers

tightening around Brady's erection as he let out a shaky breath. "You're kidding me. What are you, a boy scout? How can you have a body like this and not want to use it?" Ken stroked him once and licked his lips when Brady gasped. "Your body *needs* to be used. This hard cock is begging for it. No wonder he wants it."

"We made this date *because* he does," Brady reminded him, panting. "You told me to say yes."

Ken stroked his erection again and Brady's hips pumped forward helplessly. "Yes to drinks and getting information. Yes to another date where you might be introduced to his special friends. But you can't let him think he'll be getting this. Tonight or any other night."

"Dating isn't a skill I trained for, Tanaka. I'm—*oh fuck*—I'm doing the best I can."

"Stop. He can't handle it and I don't want to lose our only contact by breaking his arms when he tries to touch you."

Brady snarled and in two lightning-fast moves had Ken's cheek pressed against the stall door and his erection pressed firmly against his back. "You think *you* can handle me?"

Ken's moan was shameless. "You know I can. And you already know how good it feels."

Brady counted to ten and prayed for control. Then he counted a little more, unable to stop thinking about Ken sucking his cock in the bathroom. He wanted it. Was desperate for it. But they couldn't. "I have to go back out there and finish this date. And even though *he* treats me like a prostitute who wants to go legit and star in a porno, I'm *not* going to prove him right and get off in a public restroom while he pays for my drinks. I'm not that guy."

"You're having water."

"Not the point." Brady rocked against him once. Twice. "We can't do this, Tanaka, and you know it. I'm on the job you asked me to do. Just the job. That's it. That's all this is." He moved away with a wince and looked down at his steel-hard erection. "Now I have to think about deconstructed meatloaf so I can button my jeans back up. I think we can both agree that the last thing I need is Cal Grimes believing he turns me on. And then I have to find a way to introduce my favorite topic into the conversation, because *of course* part of the job is to make him think I could be interested in kink, since Burke's notes were painfully clear on that point."

He forced himself back into his pants and swore. "This might be the worst date I could ever imagine pretending to be on. I'm *so glad* I took this job."

"Brady?" Ken sounded thoughtful.

"What?" Despite everything he'd just said, if Ken asked to touch him again, Brady would give in.

"He knows you were at Burke's party before the arrest. Stephen got a lot of credit for that, so you need to prove you're serious about your interest. Just tell him you were too overwhelmed to know anything else was going on. Tell him you never thought you would like kink until you saw a demonstration that intrigued you. Tell him you haven't been able to stop thinking about it since then. That you want it, but you're afraid of wanting it at the same time because it's either too dangerous, or the fantasy will end up being better than the reality."

Brady stepped away and studied Ken's profile. He might as well have been reading his mind because he'd just described Brady's feelings—not about kink—about Ken. "That sounds good. Thanks."

He adjusted his clothes as best as he could and reached around Ken to open the door. "Are you going to stick around in case I actually do get roofied?"

Ken looked into his eyes and Brady swore his damn heart stuttered. "I'm not going anywhere, Finn. We're a team."

CHAPTER FOUR

Brady left the office he'd been crashing in wearing only sweatpants and sneakers to head down to the gym. His body was buzzing with excess energy and irritation and he needed to let off some steam. Maybe lift some weights or let his frustrations out on Ken's punching bag.

He paused at the door to the loft and lifted his fist, stopping before he could knock. That was a bad idea. Brady wouldn't exactly be great company right now. He hadn't been since that night at Tango's, and Ken Tanaka was the reason why.

While he'd secretly hoped Ken would take the lead again when they got home and kiss him until he forgot his name, a part of him had been glad to get the space he'd asked for. Ken hadn't even argued when Brady insisted on sleeping in the office, unwilling to spend the night in the loft's large bed, wishing he wasn't alone. But it quickly became clear the next day that space was all he was going to get from now on. That Ken was fine with focusing on "just the job."

Brady wasn't handling it as well.

Ken had done this after the reception too. No calls or texts. No word for over a month. Only now Brady was living with him. Eating with him. Planning his next date with Cal or trying to ignore Ken's tactical advice when he led a military campaign on an alien world.

Owen would have been jealous of Ken's game collection. Brady was jealous of his poker face.

It didn't seem fair that he'd been suffering with the pain of a near constant erection while Ken seemed as serene and unaffected as ever. It was as if their groping session in the men's room never happened. As if he didn't want what Brady did every time they were in the same room.

Was it his damn club training? Had he learned how to flip a switch and turn off his desire? Maybe he should take that class. It had been a week, and between the lack of sleep and his severe case of blue balls, Brady wasn't sure he was going to survive. The man was making him crazy.

He's giving you what you asked for.

Well, he didn't have to make it look so fucking easy.

It didn't help that the other man in his life had gone around the bend in the other direction. Three dates in and Cal was on his way to graduating from obsessed to insane.

He called Brady throughout the day just to say hello, and called every night to see if he'd changed his mind about coming over to his house to spend the night. Ken hadn't mentioned sex again but Cal couldn't seem to stop. He begged for Brady's measurements or a picture of him naked, followed him to the bathroom every time they were out just to catch a glimpse. Once, in the middle of a boring conversation about poll numbers that Brady was only half paying attention to, he realized too late that Cal had been doing more than talking on the other end of the line. And then he'd sent a picture of the outcome.

Brady grimaced. You'd think someone neck deep in politics would have learned the value of discretion. Unfortunately for him, Cal had missed that class because he was too busy jacking off. Brady swore if the man sent him one more picture of his penis, one more Vine of him sucking on popsicles, or one more link to a video of someone in a kink club being rogered and dragged around in a collar, he was going to tell Ken he quit and use the rest of his savings on a hypnotherapist. He didn't necessarily believe that he *could* be hypnotized, but he'd seen things he didn't want to remember and was willing to give it a try.

Unfortunately he couldn't quit because Ken's plan was working. Brady's hints about Burke's weekend love fest, his lies about wanting to experiment with kink—it all worked. When Cal mentioned he had important friends who threw regular parties—exclusive parties—in a private club, Ken was sure they'd hit the jackpot.

Brady let Cal believe he would be "grateful" to go. It made him ill, but he didn't want to take the chance he'd change his mind. After this party, his part would be over. He wouldn't have to put any of them through this torture anymore. Brady didn't deserve it. And Cal, no matter how he behaved, didn't deserve to be teased. He just hoped the man they were looking for was there.

He couldn't think of anything he wanted to do less than go to another elite BDSM gangbang, this time on Clingy Cal's arm. But in two days that was exactly what he was going to do, because no matter how tense and unsettled things felt between them, this was important to Ken.

Brady got the feeling Ken knew the guy they were trying to find. That they were close and that the cross he'd been wearing around his neck was somehow connected. Had one of his lovers gotten caught up with this crowd of Burke doppelgängers Ken had described?

He wished Ken would tell him. His living space might be like an open book but Tanaka was still a mystery. Who did he care about? What did he do when he wasn't playing hero or tying someone up in knots?

Brady got to the second floor, opened the stairwell door and stopped when he realized Ken was already in the gym. And he wasn't alone.

"It's the wrist flick I can't get the hang of," the man sighed, looking down at the leather whip dangling from his fingers. "I can pick a lock in under a minute but I can't manage this damn flick."

Brady narrowed his eyes on the visitor in his late thirties. He was wearing a wrinkled shirt and jeans that were faded from use, not design. His forearms were covered in old-school tattoos and his dark blond hair was a little too long and thoughtlessly mussed, as if he'd brushed it with his fingers. His beard however, was a little too neatly trimmed to match the transient vibe he'd been going for.

The man stilled and turned his head to meet Brady's gaze head on. His eyes were a soul-piercing green and highly intelligent. He was handsome beneath the mess, Brady knew. Gorgeous really, but you wouldn't see it unless you gave him a second look. It was his version of camouflage.

"Hey, Trick."

"Brady. I didn't know you were staying with Tanaka."

"Yes, you did."

"Yeah. I did."

Tristan "Trick" Dunham was an old friend from Stephen Finn's misspent youth. He'd done some time, but he'd used it wisely, getting a degree and doing his best to stay out of trouble. He was a private detective now, and loving every minute of it. Not too long ago, when Jennifer Finn was sowing her oats at that double-damned BDSM club everyone Brady knew was a member of, Stephen had hired Trick to tail her. Just to keep her safe.

Trick had loved his new assignment a little too much.

He'd been hanging around and keeping an eye on Jen ever since, but Brady was willing to bet he no longer reported his actions to Stephen.

"Whip, eh?"

Trick winked at him, then shrugged. "It was a thought, but I'm more of a traditionalist. There's nothing this baby can do that a strong, willing hand can't do better."

Ken moved closer and Brady frowned when he barely acknowledged his presence. "I'd disagree, but the way you hold my whip makes me nervous."

"Yeah, Trick. I think the last thing you want to do is hurt someone." If he'd been thinking about using that on his cousin, there might be a problem. "Speaking of mistakes, taking any classes at the college this semester, old man?"

Trick nodded, grinning at the threat beneath the question. "Auditing a few. And education is never a mistake, Marine. In fact, I'm learning a lot about dysfunctional family dynamics this go-round, so I'm here if you ever need to talk about your childhood. The middle son who kept growing so he would be seen, etcetera."

Brady's fists clenched and Ken patted Trick on the

shoulder in a way that was clearly meant to end the conversation. "I appreciate your help, Trick. And you can take the whip if you want, but don't use it until you can come back here and give me a demonstration of your skill."

Trick laughed, handing it back to Ken instead. "You lifestylers have so many rules, you never have time for fun." He nodded to Brady. "*He* knows I'm right, don't you, big guy? He's been here a week or so, right? Big boy doesn't look like he's had any fun at all. Have you let Tanaka do his Shibari voodoo on you yet? I hear it's relaxing."

"Brady's not into kink, Trick. Which you know." Now Ken's voice held the warning.

Trick was oblivious. "Neither am I, in the strictest sense. You'll never see me in leather and latex begging for my turn on the pain machine. The things I enjoy are meant for private parties and take a lot longer than a few hours every Thursday night. In my opinion, dirty is good, but kinky is complicated. Club kink, at any rate."

He looked between Brady and Ken and shook his head, his knowing smile begging to be knocked off. "I can feel a lot of sexual tension in this room. Unfortunately it's not directed at me so I think it's time for me to leave. We'll talk later. Try not to have any fun until you can give *me* a demonstration. I do like to watch, and fair is fair."

Brady watched him disappear, feeling the tic pulsing at his temple. He'd already been in a bad mood, but Trick had managed to make it worse. He didn't want to think about Jen getting mixed up with someone like him. She was back on track, back in school and taking a break from the experimenting that had led to her brush with the law. Trick wasn't a criminal, but he wasn't someone to take lightly. And he wasn't good enough for Little Finn. But then, most of the family was in agreement that no one was.

Ken stepped in front of him and laid a hand on his arm. "You know he's all talk. He likes yanking your chain, that's all."

The touch of his fingers sent a pulse of current up Brady's spine. He took a step away to break the contact. "Everyone seems to enjoy that lately. Why was he here?"

Ken hesitated, then grabbed a water bottle and took a long drink, which was when Brady noticed the sheen that still covered his chest. He'd been working out. Trick must have interrupted him.

Brady wanted to lick the salt off his skin.

"Just a favor," Ken said with a shrug. "He owes me more than one. Anyway, it's not important. I have news. This morning I made sure that I'll be doing a rope demo for the get-together. Once Cal told you where he was taking you, I made some quiet inquiries. The place is highly secure and private and prefers their own Doms as a rule. In fact, the only name I recognized is more hardcore than most, which made it harder to get in than it should have been. I had to make a few promises and twist a few arms to be put on the list, but we're good to go. You won't be alone, which is a good thing. I don't trust places I can't vet thoroughly."

What had he done for Trick to get those favors? And who had he made promises to? Brady shook his head. He was seriously fucked up.

Marine heal thyself. What had he said in that video about acting like a jealous fishwife? What did he care?

"Who are you going to be hogtying this time for our deviant audience?"

Jesus, just stop talking.

Ken sent him a questioning look. "Someone I've worked with before who knows how to put on a good show. He's a professional dancer. Why? Did *you* want to volunteer?"

Brady walked over to the leg press machine and started adding weight. "You already know I don't. Maybe this dancer could be your partner in crime instead so you don't need me to come with Cal. I think I did my part, right? We know where they're going to be? With your skills at arm twisting, I'm sure you could get everything you needed on your own."

He was being a difficult bastard and he knew it.

"What the hell, Finn? You know I can't. I won't be able to get near the target, but you'll be introduced. Vargas is our ticket to ending this. You'll shake his hand, and then you'll be done. That's what you want, right?" Ken strode over to him and dug his fingers into Brady's forearm. "Why are you trying to back out now? Is it Cal?"

He hadn't been planning on it, but Ken's reaction— no longer so serene—pushed him to continue. Brady gripped Ken's wrist firmly and dragged his hand away. "I don't know, Tanaka. Maybe I'm not the right guy to play bait, even for a good cause. Leading people on is obviously a *fetish* of yours, but I don't enjoy it. Even with a freak like Cal. God, especially him. Once this job is over, things will go back to normal for you, but I'll be dealing with the fallout for a while." He shook his head, turning back to the weights.

He'd have to warn Stephen. And stop using a traceable phone. And go to church to do penance for being such a jackass.

He didn't see it coming. He felt a rush of air and then his feet were no longer beneath him and his back was slamming hard on the gym floor, stealing his breath.

Tanaka had swept his damn legs out from under him.

Ken straddled his waist, his braid brushing Brady's chest and his amber eyes burning gold. "You think *I'm* leading *you* on? Is that what you told yourself?"

"Tanaka—"

"Who's the real tease, Finn? The way you watch me every time I look away. The way you respond every time I touch you. Willingly participate just long enough to get me rock hard before you push me away with your no-kink excuse. That's what it is, Brady. An excuse."

Brady started to move and Ken used his hands to hold his shoulders down. "Let me finish. Have I ever asked to tie you up or whip you? No. But you don't seem to care about that. It never occurred to *you* to ask why I'm in the life, or how much it does or doesn't have to do with sex, because you've already decided. You never considered that I might be drawn to you. That I might like being with you. That I might just want to have my brains fucked out by a tall, well-hung Marine whose body drives me wild."

Brady swallowed and licked his lips, his adrenaline pumping. Ken wasn't wrong. He'd never asked because he didn't want to know. It was a wall he could put up to protect himself. Four letters to stop him in his tracks. BDSM. It kept him from acting on his own darker desires. Kept him from losing himself to the chemistry between them. But now Ken was attempting to strip those excuses away, leaving Brady vulnerable. Exposed.

He bucked his hips up and twisted, flinging Ken to the floor beside him. Rolling quickly, he pinned Ken down with one arm behind his back and his hips trapped beneath Brady's erection. "What about you? You could have offered to tell me. But you leave me twisting instead. You leave me to guess how you feel, what we're really doing on this job, everything. First you suck my cock and then disappear for a month. Then you send me a text, but it's only so I can use my *giant ginger* charms to help you on a job that makes me the focus of a pervert's unwavering attention. You corner me in a restroom stall, hint at kinky role-play sessions that start just like this, and then you treat me like the invisible roommate until I piss you off."

"I didn't know he'd be that crazy."

Brady sighed. "I know. But that's the only thing I'm sure of."

"You want to know all my secrets, Finn?"

I want to know you. "It would be a nice change."

Brady couldn't resist moving his hips against Ken's, then doing it again when he heard the man beneath him moan.

"I'll give you one right now," Ken panted. "It's your secret too. I know you watched me in the shower that first morning. I know what you saw. You think I wouldn't notice the camera angle?"

Brady froze. Ken knew about that? When had he found out?

"Did you wish it was your thick dick that was stretching my ass instead of that dildo?" Ken asked, his voice a sexual challenge. "I did. I was riding it and knowing it wouldn't be enough. I wanted it to be you."

"Stop…" But Brady didn't mean it.

"Did you come, Finn? Were you watching me fuck myself and stroking that hard cock? Or is that too kinky for a guy like you to admit to? I told you I wanted you.

Do you have the balls to tell me what you want?"

Rising off him, Brady reached for the waistband of the loose black pants Ken was wearing and dragged them down and off, throwing them over his shoulder. He dragged Ken up to a standing position in front of him and cupped his jaw with trembling fingers. "You want me again?"

"I always want you, Brady. I was trying to give you space."

"No space." He was too turned on to argue. "Just sex. No toys or restraints or mind games, and I'm the one inside you. Give me your word and I'll trust it." More than he trusted himself right now.

Ken's addictive lips parted for a short, shaky breath. "Anything you want, Finn. I've waited too long to care about anything else. Just fuck me."

"Upstairs." Brady bit out before lifting Ken off his feet and walking toward the service elevator. "Does this work?"

"Everything works."

Good. He didn't think he could let Ken go long enough to race up one flight of stairs. He didn't have the strength.

He pushed the button as Ken wrapped his long, agile

legs around him, pressing his erection against Brady's stomach and lowering his mouth for a kiss. Brady groaned as Ken sucked on his tongue the way he'd sucked his cock. Hungry. Greedy. God, he never wanted it to stop.

Inside the elevator, Ken pushed Brady's sweatpants down with his feet. Without lifting his mouth, Brady toed off his sneakers and stepped out of his clothes. Finally. *This.* Skin to skin. He didn't want anything between them that didn't have to be.

The door opened with a soft *ding* and Brady walked blindly, praying he was going in the right direction.

Ken lifted his mouth and gasped. "Here. Do it here."

"Lube," he croaked. "Condom."

Ken moaned and pressed his face into Brady's neck, licking and biting the sensitive flesh, making Brady shudder. "Top drawer in the bathroom."

They managed to turn the knob on the loft door together, swinging it open while Brady made a beeline for that top drawer. He had to get inside Ken. He couldn't think of anything else.

Brady set him down beside the bed and let him go, turning for the bathroom. "Top drawer?"

Before Ken could respond, Brady was rifling through

varying sizes and flavors of condoms and lubes. *So many,* he thought wildly. *Where did he get... I just need—there.* Regular lube and the right sized condom. Hallelujah.

He came out with his hands full and found Ken waiting for him with flushed cheeks and swollen lips. Grabbing Brady's arm, he dropped to his knees, taking them both down to the floor.

Brady glanced at the bed beside them and Ken chuckled raggedly. "You got me all worked up in the gym, Finn. Pinning me to the floor like that. I loved it. I want you to fuck me right here."

Fuck yes.

Ken set the lube down beside them and took the condom out of Brady's hand.

Tearing it open, he bent his head and swiftly mouthed the tip of Brady's erection before rolling the latex down with expert fingers.

It took all of Brady's control to let him finish. As soon as Ken let go, Brady was on him, kissing him and sliding his sheathed erection against Ken's hard shaft.

God, yes. Need you. Need you so much. I'll be careful. I'll make it so good...

Ken bit Brady's lip until he tasted blood, making him

snarl and lift his head to see the sparkle of desire and mischief in those golden eyes. "I promised no toys, but you have to promise something too."

Anything. "What?"

"Don't hold back."

He didn't know what he was asking. "Tanaka, I—"

Ken pressed one finger to his lips. "I took you down in the gym and I can do it again. I know pressure points that could put you in the fetal position. I could stop you if you were hurting me. I can take you, Brady Finn. So take me."

Jesus, that was hot. His words caused something inside Brady to burst apart. He caught Ken's surprised expression before he twisted him around, pressing his chest to the floor. Brady spread Ken's ass cheeks roughly and poured a liberal amount of lube between them, his mouth watering and cock twitching at the sight of the tight little hole being readied for him.

"This is what I wanted to do," he rasped, hardly recognizing his voice as fantasy merged with reality. "In the shower. I wanted to throw you on the floor and fuck you. Make you scream my name. Make you come."

A fine tremor shook Ken's lean body beneath his hands and he lifted up onto his elbows, his ass tilting enticingly. "Do it, Brady. I need it. Make me scream."

Jesus. Brady gripped Ken's hip and guided his cock to that tight ring of muscles that clenched in anticipation. Would he hurt him? "Tell me if you need me to stop."

Brady hissed as he pushed the head of his shaft inside and felt Ken's muscles squeeze around him like a vise. "Fuck, you're tight. Damn it, I've never felt anything so ti— We need to slow down…"

He heard Ken breathe out with a low moan, and then Brady was shouting in shock and arousal as Ken backed up forcefully, impaling and stretching himself wide on Brady's cock. "*Fuck.*"

"*Yes.*" Ken cried. "Oh God, you're so big. Fuck me, Finn. Make me take it. I need it so bad."

Brady bent over Ken's back, one hand digging into his shoulder and the other wrapping around his braid as he started to move inside him. *Deeper.* "You like that?" He yanked the braid and Ken cried out. "Damn, that's sexy, Tanaka. Do it again." Another yank and another cry of arousal.

He dragged his hips back, grinding his teeth with the effort of restraint. Such a tight fit. He wouldn't last long, but he never wanted to stop.

He'd never imagined it would feel like this. That sex

could feel like this. Like dying and being born again with every thrust of his hips. It felt so good it hurt. So good he forced himself to pick out a tattoo on Ken's back he could focus on in case he started losing control. He wanted to make this last.

"Brady." Ken moaned low, shuddering. "Harder. Your cock is in me so deep, everywhere, and I'm so close. Fuck me harder so I can come."

He hadn't even touched him yet. Brady's hand left his hip to grip Ken's erection. It was already dripping with pre-cum. Ken shuddered again at the touch and Brady's fingers were coated. Holy shit. "Can you come like this, Ken? If I give you the hard fucking you're begging for, will you come for me?"

"Need to come for you. Want you so bad. Make me…" Ken sounded lost in pleasure. Brady couldn't resist him. Not now.

He dropped Ken's braid and held onto his other shoulder, the wet fingers of his other hand firmly on Ken's stomach. He took a deep breath that was more like a prayer before increasing his rhythm. *Faster.* He heard the slap of their flesh with each quick thrust and grit his teeth as lightning started to spark up his spine.

God, that's it. You love it don't you, you sexy

bastard? Love having that tight hole fucked and filled so much you're going to come before I do.

Ken cried out his approval when Brady started to sling his hips forward with more force. It felt so good he had to go deeper. Harder.

Harder. Pin him to the floor and fuck him. That was what Ken wanted. That was what Brady was desperate to give him.

The large room rang with their hoarse cries as he set a jarring, punishing rhythm. Ken's tight ass stretched around him, trying to accommodate his girth, and seeing it made Brady wilder. Soon his hips were banging into Ken's so hard and fast that the man beneath him started clawing at the wood floor for purchase. "Is that too hard, Ken? Too much? Are you going to try and stop me now?" *Don't tell me to stop.*

"Don't stop, Finn," he begged hoarsely. "That's it. Like that. Oh, that big cock is fucking me *so hard*. It's perfect. *Give me more*."

Brady started to growl with each impact, hearing Ken begging for him. For more. It *was* perfect. Raw. He'd never let go like this before. Never taken what he really wanted without holding back. This was what he needed. *And Ken wanted more.*

Ken's hand reached for his where it had flattened on his stomach. "Coming." His words were garbled with arousal. "I'm coming for you, Brady. Coming hard for you."

Brady gripped Ken's cock and felt each pulsing wave as he ejaculated onto the floor. "*Christ*, Ken, I—"

Knowing he was coming without help made Brady so hot that he fell over the edge. He pressed Ken's shoulders down flat on the floor and filled him over and over again as he found his climax, shouting his name and falling into oblivion. "Ken. *God, Tanaka*. Ken... Oh, fuck!"

Lightning struck and he couldn't hear anything but his own heart. Couldn't feel anything but Ken's tight ass milking his release as he rocked against him.

They both collapsed onto their sides, still connected as they rode the rough aftershocks together. Ken pushed back into him like a cat in need of stroking and Brady lifted one weak arm to caress his hip. He was glad he hadn't hurt him. The man beside him was practically humming with pleasure and release, removing all his doubts.

Brady had come so hard his body was nearly boneless, but his mind was already reeling from shock.

What the *hell* just happened?

Great sex.

Not strong enough. He couldn't find the right words to describe the heights he'd just reached, what he'd felt when Ken... Was that normal for him? He knew he touched himself when he was alone in the shower, but he hadn't needed to with Brady. Could he do that with all his lovers? Brady didn't want to ask, didn't want to know if other men had gotten that reaction. This belonged to him.

In thirty-four years he'd had five relationships, including his first time in the back of the minivan his date had borrowed from his mother. He admitted to not being as experienced as...well, ninety-eight percent of his male relatives, but he enjoyed sex and loved orgasms as much as everyone else.

What had just happened with Ken was another level, another galaxy, from anything he knew. And as the knot formed in his stomach, he realized that most of his other reasons for putting Ken off had been bullshit. This was why he'd resisted. Somehow he'd known that having him would change things forever. Change *him*. That he would never want to give it up, and that nothing less would ever be enough.

Just sex, he'd told him. But it felt like more. It felt like everything.

CHAPTER FIVE

He woke up shouting in horror. Pain. Shock. Men and women were running toward him on fire, the smell of charred flesh all around him.

"Brady, wake up. You're dreaming. Just a dream."

Ken was here, nearly on top of him, as if he'd been trying to hold Brady down.

A dream. Already fading. Just a memory. Brady forced himself to stop struggling. "I'm awake. You can let me go."

As soon as Ken released him Brady threw back the covers and got to his feet. He headed for the bathroom sink to splash cool water on his face and slow his racing heart. *Only a bad dream. You're home. It's over. Let it go.*

He wished it were that easy. Wished he could fall back into Ken's arms and go to sleep without seeing those images burned in his mind. But that wasn't going to happen now.

They'd spent the entire day in the loft exploring each other. Again and again they'd given in to the need that only got stronger each time. Again and again Ken had proven to be the most creative and passionate lover Brady could have asked for. His body was incredibly responsive. As addicting as his mouth.

The sex had been so mind altering that he'd actually forgotten about his nighttime handicap and fallen asleep. He never thought about how his nightmares would affect someone sleeping in the same bed. Had he physically lashed out in his effort to escape? Had he hurt Ken?

He saw Ken's reflection in the mirror, his hair loose and flowing down his back in a way that made Brady's breath catch. "I'm really sorry I woke you. What time is it?"

"Three-thirty. And don't worry about it. Are you okay?"

He used the hand towel to dry his face and forced a smile. "Just a bad dream. It happens. You should go back to bed. I'm going to grab something cool to drink."

And go back across the hall so I don't wake you when it happens again.

When he got to the kitchen he realized Ken was still behind him. "How often?"

"What?" He poured a glass of water, wanting to do anything but talk about this.

Ken pushed his hair back away from his face and watched him with knowing eyes. "How often does it happen? Once a month? Once a week?"

Every night since he'd come home, with the exception of the Great Rumming of 2015, when he didn't dream at all. He supposed getting blackout-drunk had benefits, but he wouldn't trade one problem for another. "Unless you have a swampy tea for bad dreams, it doesn't really matter, does it? Anyway I'm told they'll fade in time. Seriously, Tanaka, go back to bed."

Ken sent him a speaking look. "Just because you broke my body with your big hard cock doesn't mean you can boss me around. I'll go to bed when I feel like it, preferably with one hand tangled in that sexy red chest hair and yours on my ass."

Brady licked his lips, his cock stirring as he stared at Ken's body. There were bruises on his hips and arms that made Brady frown, but Ken kept assuring him he wasn't hurt. And he was vocal enough about his pleasure that there was no way Brady could doubt it. "If you're staying awake too, I'm always up for another round of body breaking."

Ken shook his head. "On the couch. Now."

He went to sit down, sighing heavily. He didn't like talking about it. Jeremy had caught him wandering around the house in the middle of the night that first week and Brady had tried to make light of it, but he could tell the man had been genuinely concerned. He'd tried to convince Brady to talk to someone about it, but in some ways he couldn't avoid being his father's son. Pride kept him from seeing a therapist. Pride kept him from telling his brothers. Pride told him he just needed to suck it up and wait it out. To be a man.

Pride was a chatty little son of a bitch.

"Look, I'm fine, Tanaka. I usually only sleep a few hours a night. The Marines don't give you a lot of time to work on your napping skills."

Ken sat down in his lap, his bare ass pressed against Brady's thickening shaft while he stared him down. "I appreciate how bad you are at lying, but you don't need to bother. Not with me."

"I'm not lying when I tell you your ass is distracting

me. But don't move. I like it."

Ken didn't move. "I like it too, Finn. I like everything about this. Except the part where you woke up screaming. Have you talked to someone?"

"I'm talking to you right now," Brady responded swiftly. "I've talked to Jeremy. I don't really see the point in talking to a stranger about something only time can fix."

"Stubborn. Is it the red hair? Or the Finn in you?"

"Unless you want some Finn in *you*, we should talk about something else."

Ken's smile was tinged with a sadness that tugged at Brady's heart. "Okay then. I'll share. I think it's time I told you about the man we're looking for. The reason I've put you through that Cal torture and not kicked his ass and called it a day. His name is Terry. Terry Wahl."

He'd wanted Ken to offer up some information. Now his stomach was in knots, not knowing what Ken would say. "He's a friend?"

"He should have been. And I should have told you about him from the beginning, but I'm not used to sharing that part of my life with anyone."

Brady lifted his hand to the artwork on Ken's back, tracing the designs and trying not to push. "How do you know him?"

"His mother Patricia took me in after my parents died." Ken leaned into him and Brady pulled him closer, aching for his loss. "She was my father's secretary. After the accident, when she realized there was no family at the funeral and no one willing to come for me, she filed the paperwork to become my foster mother. I lived with her and her two boys until I was old enough to claim my trust fund."

"And were you happy there?"

"I liked *her*," Ken evaded. "I was fifteen, grieving and angry at being abandoned. I was obsessed with games and electronics even then, so that helped. They were easier to deal with than people. Than thinking about what I'd lost. If I could understand a machine, I could fix it. I used to take Patricia's computer apart once a week. It drove her up the wall."

It would have been tough to keep up with Tanaka as a teen. "She was a single mom?"

Ken grinned. "She said a husband was a distraction she couldn't afford with three boys and a job. She also said men were usually only good for one thing, and then only in the first month of the relationship before they got complacent. She never said that to *us* of course, but I used to eavesdrop through the vents on Scrabble night when her girlfriends came over."

Brady laughed and adjusted himself discreetly. He was completely focused on the conversation, but his body kept reminding him that Ken was naked. "She sounds like quite a woman."

"She was. She is." Ken touched the cross around his neck. "And I can't let her down again."

Again?

"You didn't let her down."

Ken's laugh held no humor. "You don't know that."

"I know you. You'd never do anything to—"

"I left them," Ken interrupted. "When I got my money, I left for school and had never looked back. My teachers thought I was a genius and I was in love with a tall California cowboy with a fetish for rope. I was living the dream."

In love? "There's nothing wrong with that. You were young. Why shouldn't you want to have fun?" He'd been in love with a *cowboy?*

Get a fucking grip, Brady.

"I said the same thing. I told myself it was fine because I'd done the math and given Patricia a sum equal to the cost of raising a teenage boy for three years.

I sent her Christmas cards. What I didn't do was call or try to get together with her or the boys for the next thirteen years."

"People drift apart. I'm sure if they'd needed you—"

"She probably needed me the day Dale was sent home from Iraq in a box. But I didn't even know the boys had enlisted."

"Oh, hell, Ken. That's…" He honestly didn't know what to say. Jesus.

"Exactly." Ken slid off his lap and grabbed the throw from the back of the couch to wrap around his waist. Brady surreptitiously slid a pillow onto his lap. "Finn Club is looking pretty damn good right now, isn't it? No matter what happens or what you've been through, none of you would ever think about abandoning your family. Even the family yours basically adopted, like Tasha and Jeremy."

"Not true. I think a few of us have had moments where we wished we didn't have to deal with the Finn clan. Didn't have so many people to answer to. I know *I've* thought about leaving," Brady admitted softly, feeling the need to ease Ken's guilt. "I came home and every familiar face reminded me of what I'd lost. That the guy they knew was gone and I was a fraud. If

Stephen hadn't hired me, if Owen and Jeremy hadn't let me basically move in without asking... I might have started over somewhere else and never looked back."

Ken sat down on the coffee table across from him and put his hand on Brady's thigh. "Remind me that I owe them one."

Squeezing Brady's knee, Ken picked up the thread of his story. "A few years ago I realized my mistake and got in touch with Patricia. Terry was still enlisted, so I made sure to call her every week and get together for dinner a few times a month so she wouldn't be alone. She was wary at first. I guess that's why she didn't tell me Terry was home right away. She was protecting him until he got on his feet. The doctors at the VA said he was suffering from PTSD."

He sent Brady a look that said *just like you* before continuing.

"He had nightmares every night. He stopped sleeping completely for a while and she said he'd look right through her, as if he were seeing something else. Then he seemed to balance out. He'd gotten back on his meds and met a man, he told her. A wealthy man who spoiled him and promised he'd take care of him. He thought it was love."

Brady could feel the anger rising inside him. "Vargas?"

"No. Richards was the first man's name. But I think...I think from the files that these men like to pass their toys around. Those phrases I couldn't figure out? I finally cracked it a few days ago. Burke kept track of that with his own cypher since he procured more than one companion for them over the years, all of them young and strong. All of them lost and malleable. It was his way of keeping them in his pocket."

"Motherfucker."

"We're close," Ken murmured. "If I'm right, and I think I am, Vargas was the last to trade with Richards. That has to mean he has Terry or knows where he is."

He hesitated. "I've hated putting you in this position, Brady. I hate that you've had to deal with a man like Grimes, and that your second experience with BDSM might be worse than the first. If there was any other way..."

"I know there isn't," Brady assured him.

"If we can get Terry back, I have the money and Trick knows people who can help him and Patricia disappear. Protect them until I can send those bastards where they belong."

"We. Until *we* can send those bastards where they belong." Brady covered Ken's hand with his own. "Thank you for telling me. I'm in this now and I promise you, we'll get Terry back to his mother."

"Thank you. No more talking about this." Ken undid the blanket and stood, tangling his fingers with Brady's. "Come with me."

Brady had no desire to resist. He felt protective of Ken for the first time since he'd known him. He'd seemed so independent. Almost too perfect. But he was as messed up as everybody else. It made him more beautiful.

When they reached the bathroom, Ken squeezed his hand and let it go. "Don't move."

Brady watched him open a drawer in his dresser and take out a folded piece of paper. He walked over and handed it to him. "Read it."

He looked down at the test results, understanding making his heart race. "This was done over four months ago."

"Right after we met," Ken agreed. "I can take it again tomorrow, but I haven't been with anyone but you since then."

He hadn't? Something powerful and possessive

swept through Brady. "Same here. And I got tested as soon as I came home."

Brady tried to read his expression and Ken just smiled his fallen-angel smile. "I know."

He frowned suspiciously. "You know?"

Ken braided and wrapped his hair in a bun, watching him. "I was curious. Don't focus on it. Focus on the fact that we don't need anything between us in the shower. That I don't want anything between us. Focus on the fact that I have *never* said that before. Until you."

All the blood rushed to his cock so fast it made him dizzy. He dropped the paper, came in and leaned against the sink while Ken started the shower. Brady's gaze lingered on the tattoos on his back and he couldn't resist reaching out to touch. They were done in black and stylized in such a way that they'd been hard to decipher at first glance, but on closer inspection, he could see a koi fish swirling around a dragon—the dragon's tail went down his arm and in its claw was a lotus. It was beautifully done.

"What do they mean? The fish and the dragon?"

Ken stood, looking at him over his shoulder. "For me it's about becoming more than I was yesterday. Learning from my mistakes and moving forward."

"They're sexy as hell."

"That too."

Ken stepped into the shower and let it soak him, reminding Brady how much he'd wanted to be with him the last time he saw him like this.

He followed Ken into the stall. "I really love this shower," he muttered. "We both fit."

"I've always had a thing for big men," Ken admitted as he moved over to the long stone bench and sat down, looking up at Brady through his thick, dark lashes. "I'm told I'm particular. Big, strong redheads with delicious cocks are my current obsession."

Ken licked his lips and Brady moved closer, gripping the base of his erection. "Is this what you wanted? In particular?"

"All the time." Ken caressed Brady's thighs and hips, his amber eyes bright and fixed on the thick shaft in front of him. "I got so turned on the first time I took you in my mouth. You were so big and I wanted you to come in my mouth so much I nearly came myself before you stopped me. It's almost embarrassing how easy I am when it comes to you."

Brady swore. Thinking about Ken coming made him impatient. "Don't tell me how much you like it. Show me."

He liked that. Brady could see it in his eyes. "Yes, sir."

Ken tightened his fingers on Brady's hips and opened his mouth over his waiting erection. Brady guided it in, watching those addictive lips, that magical mouth stretch wide as he filled it.

Oh, that's beautiful. That's so good. You can take me. Every fucking inch.

Ken moaned and leaned forward as if he'd accepted the unspoken challenge. He reached out and took Brady's hands and put them on his head, telling him without words what he wanted.

He was putting Brady in control.

"Fuck," Brady gasped, his fingers curling around the braided bun, palms cupping the back of Ken's head. "I don't want to…" *Hurt you. I don't want to give you more than you can take.*

Ken groaned and took more, his tongue swirling around Brady's shaft, making his thighs tremble from the restraint.

He wants it.

So did Brady. His grip tightened and he started to rock his hips forward, pushing his shaft deeper into

Ken's mouth. He could already feel the tip pressing against the back of his lover's throat.

"I love your mouth," Brady groaned. "The noises you make. The way your… I want to fuck it. Is that what you're trying to tell me? Is that what you want?"

Ken nodded and made a sound of pleasure as he swallowed.

"*Yes.*" Need overpowered his control too quickly for him to react. To stop his hips from pumping a little deeper and his hands from tugging that hot mouth forward with each thrust. "*God, yes.* Fucking your hot mouth. Oh damn, Ken, that's good. Taking me down deep. Damn—"

He couldn't talk anymore. He couldn't think. All he could do was watch Ken take everything he gave him, his mouth so full and stretched that tears were filling his eyes. Brady wanted to claim it, mark it with his release and watch Ken swallow him down. But he wanted something else more.

Brady let go of Ken's hair and stepped back with a shudder, spinning around to turn off the shower.

"What are you doing? Why did you stop me again?" Ken's voice was raw from Brady's rough treatment.

That shouldn't have turned him on.

He answered by picking Ken up with his arms around his ribs and carrying him with his feet inches off the floor until they reached the side of the bed. Then he tossed him back on those thin, cloud-like sheets.

"Damn it, Finn, we'll soak the sheets."

Brady didn't care. He reached for the bottle of lube and slid his hands under Ken's damp thighs, spreading and pushing until his knees were pressed against his shoulders.

He loved how flexible Ken was. He wanted to bend and twist and take him in every position he could find. He just wanted Ken, any way he could have him.

"What are you doing?" Ken asked again, a little breathless now.

Coating his own erection with lube, Brady tried to smile, but his muscles felt too tight. "Making you come for me."

He pressed one lubed finger inside Ken's ass and bit his lip as those powerful muscles gripped it tight. He slid another finger inside and groaned. "You shouldn't have told me I could have it before you started teasing me in the shower."

"Have what?"

"I love your mouth, I do. But I can't get enough of

this ass, Tanaka. I want to spend hours on it. In it. And I want to feel what it's like inside with nothing between us. I want it so bad I ache."

"Don't tell me how much you like it," Ken gasped, repeating Brady's words. "Show me."

Brady pulled his fingers out in one swift move and replaced them with the head of his bare cock, making Ken gasp again.

"Are you ready for me, Tanaka?"

"I'm always ready for you."

He leaned forward until the backs of Ken's thighs were pressing against his shoulders and their mouths were only inches apart. Then he flexed the cheeks of his ass and slung his hips forward, filling Ken with one forceful stroke.

"Fuck!" Ken cried into his mouth. "Ah, God. Brady. So deep. I can feel you…"

Brady's fists were destroying the sheet on either side of Ken's head as he fought to hold himself together. "So much better," he muttered. "How can it be better?"

Ken reached up and cupped the back of Brady's head. "Kiss me and make me come, Finn."

Brady kissed him and began to rock inside him. Jesus, that was good. Ken's tongue was tangling with his as their bodies fought to get closer. He couldn't get close enough.

After a few minutes he tore his mouth away and arched his neck, dizzy and aroused and desperate for air. "What was that?"

Ken's hands had lowered to Brady's ass while their lips were locked, and he'd slipped one finger between Brady's cheeks and started to massage his clenched muscles.

"Don't stop," Ken panted. "I couldn't help it. Your tongue was in my mouth, your thick cock is in my ass and I wanted everything."

Brady took both his hands and held them over Ken's head. "I'm trying to give you everything, Tanaka. Don't distract me."

He'd loved it too much.

Having Ken completely unable to move, his legs over his shoulders and his hands over his head, made Brady wild. He'd captured his prey. He was in control. "Ken," he growled. "Ken, let me... Don't stop me."

The blood was rushing so fast in his ears that he couldn't tell if he'd gotten permission, but it was too late. He needed to fuck. He needed to claim. He dug into the bed and his hips were like pistons, pumping harder and faster and—*Oh Fuck, mine. This is mine.*

He was looking down between their bodies, watching his cock disappear into that tight hole again and again, when he heard Ken's broken shout. "*Brady.*"

Primal satisfaction seared up his spine when he saw the head of Ken's flushed cock pulse as he came. He wanted to taste it. Wanted to lick every last drop off Ken's stomach and take him in his mouth until he was ready to do it again.

But he could feel Ken's muscles pulsing and squeezing his cock as he came. It was too good. He needed to come. Nothing between them. Nothing to stop his climax from filling Ken's ass. The last thought pushed him over the edge. He let go of Ken's wrists, sliding his hands down to his slick shoulders as he came. "Inside you. Fuck, Ken, I'm coming inside you, baby." *No one else.*

"*Yes.*"

He was blind with adrenaline and ecstasy and the feeling that he was home. Right now. With Ken... "Fuck."

Ken wrapped his arms and legs around Brady, rocking him as he shook with the force of his orgasm. "That was..."

"I know."

More than he could have expected or hoped for...

And scary as hell.

CHAPTER SIX

The sounds of family surrounded him as soon as Brady walked in the door of Noah and Wyatt's townhouse—barked orders, loud conversations and laughter. All the chaos of home that he'd missed when he was overseas, and the new voices that had been added along the way. He grinned as he took it all in.

"Stephen? Grab Little Sean before you go upstairs."

"Rory, I told you to put those rolls in the oven *four times*. The roast is almost done and you're still texting this week's Romeo."

"Wyatt, Penny drew on your bathroom wall."

"Never rat out family, Jake. Your Great-Grandpa Finn learned that the hard way."

"Wyatt, do *not* tell that story to the kids."

Brady glanced over his shoulder at the wide-eyed Ken. "You still have time to escape. No one's spotted you yet."

Little Sean instantly made him a liar. "Uncle Necky!"

Brady bent down to scoop up the running three-year-old before he could reach Ken's legs. "Uncle Necky, huh? Don't *I* get a hello?"

Sean patted his cheeks with sticky hands and smiled. "'Lo, Brady." His large brown eyes turned back toward Ken and his hands went to his own shaggy black curls. "Braid," he demanded.

Stephen appeared beside them, no tie and his sleeves rolled up. Penny's twin Wes was right behind him, the little blond mimicking every move he made. "There he is. Wes and I are supposed to get him washed up for dinner, but he keeps eluding us, the slippery bugger."

"He *is* a slippery bugger," Wes agreed. Brady winked at him.

Stephen saw Tanaka and showed momentary surprise before recovering with his usual aplomb. He was a natural politician—he knew how to put people at ease. "Hey there, Ken. I didn't know you were coming to the Finn Again."

"It was last minute," Ken responded. "I hope it's not

an imposition."

Stephen laughed and shook his head. "If you're brave enough to join this mob, there's no such thing. Let me get the scamp scrubbed and we can talk more at dinner. I have something I wanted to run by Brady anyway."

Brady frowned. He did?

Stephen grabbed Little Sean from him and headed toward the bathroom before he could find out more, and he and Brady watched Sean struggling to escape the senator's grasp, shouting, "Braid! Uncle Necky! Braid!"

"Run by you later, Brady." Wes threw him the peace sign, then raced after Stephen.

Brady looked at Ken and grinned. "You did say you wanted to come, Uncle Necky. This is on you."

"I can't believe he remembers me." Ken was still staring after Sean. "I haven't seen him since Tasha's wedding."

"You made a big impression."

"I gave him cake."

Brady snorted. "Everyone gave him cake. Have you *seen* him? He's adorable and he always gets his way. Seamus said he was on a sugar high for the next day and a half."

Ken put his hand on Brady's forearm. Just a light

touch, but it felt too intimate for the family setting. "Did Stephen say this was a *Finnegan*?"

"Not Finnegan. Finn. Again. Blame Tasha. She got her way because no one else wanted monthly takeout from Ruby's."

Ken was smiling. "I know how she seriously she takes Ruby's. Why Finn Again?"

"I told you we started doing this every month, all the cousins getting together to eat and catch up?"

Ken nodded. Brady had told him how new it was. With their fathers' long, silent war, the cousins had rarely spent much time together unless they took it for themselves. Brady's move to Owen's house and job with Stephen had given them more of an excuse.

"Well, we've actually done it *twice* a month since Uncle Shawn got out of the hospital. The other meal includes our parents, which, thanks to Solomon the Elder, is awkward, short on interesting details and long on uncomfortable silence. Tasha called this one the Finn Again so we wouldn't forget which meal was which and whether or not we had to behave. I guess it stuck."

Ken's expression was bemused as he took in the chaos around him. "You do this twice a month?"

Brady's smile faltered. "It's not mandatory and it's

rarely at the same location, but yeah. More or less."

Had this been a mistake? Ken was used to a lot of space and a solitary lifestyle outside of the club. Wyatt and Noah's townhouse wasn't as small as Rory or Solomon's place, but with everyone crammed inside, it might as well have been.

He'd only mentioned the dinner because they'd both been tense about tomorrow's task and he thought Ken might get a kick out of the madness. Now he was worried it was too much. After the last few days, he didn't want to do anything to push him away.

Brady couldn't think of another relationship he'd been in where his emotions had been so complicated and intense. One minute, it felt like it was happening so fast that he wasn't even sure there'd been time to *call* it a relationship. The next it was—something. Definitely something. With potential for more.

For him it already felt like more. At night he still slipped away and slept across the hall to deal with his nightmares alone, but the rest of the time he was equal parts anxious, aroused and over the damn moon, discovering a side of himself, both in and out of the bedroom, that he'd always been afraid to explore until Tanaka.

Brady had been learning more about him as well. His parents had both been workaholics, despite their financial comfort. He had memories of traveling all over the world, but not that many of family dinners or fun. The details about his time as foster brother to the Wahls made it clear it hadn't been an easy fit for any of the boys—not just Ken. Dale and Terry had been younger and angry that Ken's presence caused so much upheaval. They'd had to share a room, their mother had had to get a new job with longer hours and Ken was too caught up in his own grief to be interesting. It set the tone for three years of thinly veiled animosity that Patricia had never seen.

It hurt Brady's heart to know that Ken had been punishing himself for something he'd had no control over. He couldn't have saved Dale from his fate, but he was doing everything in his power to save Terry so the woman who had taken him in wouldn't lose both her sons. Brady couldn't help but admire that.

Ken Tanaka had been alone for most of his life. Love interests and kink mentoring aside, he'd had no family to support him. No one to praise his accomplishments or give him hell when he was making the wrong decision.

In a small way it reminded him of Jeremy's situation.

His parents hadn't died but they might as well have, kicking him out of the house when he was fourteen, but at least he'd had Owen, Ellen and Shawn to help him heal. Ken hadn't been able to really connect with anyone apart from lovers and professors until he joined his first fetish community. People accepted him there, appreciated his talents. Gave him friendship without asking for something in return.

Ken deserved to be loved, to have family, but Brady didn't know if that was what he wanted. Tanaka had been an island for a long time. Maybe he was happy with what he had and Brady was projecting. Looking for a sign that Ken might want to be a part of his crowded, messy life.

Tomorrow Brady would have his last date with Cal, meet this Vargas guy and force himself to smile so Ken could find his foster brother. Maybe they'd get lucky and Terry would be there. Brady wasn't sure what came after that. He wasn't sure if Ken wanted anything to come after that. He hated the uncertainty.

"Brady? Is everything okay?"

He didn't get the chance to answer Ken's question because the others had seen him and finally made their way over.

"Tanaka?"

"Ken!"

"Who invited Hacker Guy to the Finn Again?"

Tasha pushed through the crowd of males and wrapped her arms around Ken with a sexy smile. The soft swell of her abdomen, only just beginning to show in her fourth month of pregnancy, made her curvy figure even more beautiful. "It's so nice to see my two heroes together again."

She leaned back in his arms and sent Brady a wink. "Hey there, Hot Body Man. What's a piece of apple pie like you doing with this salted caramel confection?"

Brady raised his eyebrow. "He's just visiting his good friend, Sugar Buns. Speaking of...how's the one in your oven?"

"I like it when you sass." She smirked and met Ken's gaze. "Can that be my new nickname in the media? Sugar Buns sounds so much sexier than *Mom-in-Waiting* or *Senator Finn's Baby Mama*."

Ken kissed her and smiled. "I thought the *Baker of the Finns* was interesting if a little cannibalistic. But for you, I'll work on Sugar Buns. You look good, Tasha."

Brady's brother Noah joined them, chuckling. "Baker of *what now*? Who pays them to write that shit?"

"Morons." Solomon nodded to Brady, his blue eyes sparkling despite his ever-present frown. "Nice to see you, Brady. I wasn't sure you'd make it. Now that you have, tell Noah to watch his mouth. Apparently Penny and Wes spent days repeating what they heard here. So did Jake. His middle school takes that kind of language seriously, even when it's a bookworm defending himself against a bully. His teacher sent him to detention."

"Is Jake being bullied?" Noah's voice lowered dangerously. "I can show him a few moves if he wants. He damn sure won't need to swear to get his point across."

Solomon sighed. "Yes, let's teach him how to fight. I'm *sure* Seamus would approve. Jackass."

Brady bit the inside of his cheek, knowing it would be a Herculean task for his brothers to get through an entire meal without swearing. They'd always blamed Salty Sol and the lack of a good female influence, but with Papa Seamus around, that excuse wasn't working anymore.

The door behind them opened and they all turned around in time to see Brady's cousin Jennifer rushing in with a large, plastic container. She blew a strand of strawberry blonde hair out of her eyes and smiled. "Am I late again?"

There was a collective gasp when the container slipped from her hands and the bisque she'd been in charge of getting from the deli splattered all over the floor, her shoes and the cuffs of her jeans. "Son of a bitch," she swore loudly, bending down to start scooping the hot soup up with her hands. "I'm so sorry. Ouch—*damn it*. I definitely need a towel for this."

"Son of a bitch!" Penny sang as she ran past them toward the kitchen, and all the men started to laugh.

"Not my fault this time," Noah chortled, towel in hand as he tugged Jen gently to her feet. "Go clean yourself up, princess. We've got this under control."

Brady frowned as she headed up the stairs. Her hands had been shaking and she looked frazzled. "What's going on with Jen?"

"Little Finn?" Tasha responded lightly. "She just spilled soup on her pants. Oh, and I think she has a test coming up. She's fine, Brady."

He narrowed his eyes on Stephen's wife. *Leave it alone.* That's what she was really saying. Which meant something was definitely up.

Was her ex-fiancé back? Someone from the club bothering her? Or was this about Trick?

Seamus distracted him by grabbing the back of Noah's collar and fast-walking with him to the kitchen. "I think something's burning in your oven, Firefighter."

Solomon flinched and then he was right behind them, shouting for Rory, who'd apparently forgotten to set a timer for the rolls.

It took forty minutes to air out the kitchen, get the table set, sit the four kids in front of the flat screen and settle everyone else around the card tables Wyatt and Noah had pushed together and covered with a brand new tablecloth. When Brady pointed out the price tag still attached to the fabric, Wyatt shrugged. "We don't like to cook. I'm just glad we didn't have to buy silverware."

Noah lifted his beer bottle in agreement. "We do, however, have enough takeout menus to live like kings. And now, thanks to this becoming a regular thing, we have something to bring back to the firehouse besides stories of debauchery and our own charming selves."

Wyatt clinked his beer bottle to Noah's. "To leftovers."

"Amen."

Solomon—seated at the head of the table—looked around the room at the others and nodded. "Let's eat."

During the few minutes that everyone was occupied

with filling their plates, Brady leaned close to Ken and whispered, "Sorry you came?"

"Hardly," he replied quietly. "I'm surrounded by gorgeous blue-eyed Irishmen who can make an ordinary dinner into an adventure. I can't remember the last time I enjoyed myself so much."

"Really, Tanaka? I can. It was only a few hours ago."

Ken paused with a spoon full of mashed potatoes hovering over his plate and Brady looked around uncomfortably. "Sorry." Had he actually been flirting with Ken in front of his family? Brady didn't flirt, and he didn't want Ken to feel awkward if he didn't want them to know. "Sorry," he mumbled again.

"Don't be." Ken passed him the bowl and their fingers touched. "I'm not."

At the other end of the table Rory noticed. "Hey now. What's going on with you two?"

Brady wanted to kiss his cousin when Seamus answered before he could. "They're on another job, I think. Like the Burke thing."

"Is *that* what's happening?" Stephen stood up to reach for a casserole dish of green beans before continuing, "Thank God. I was trying to come up with a subtle way of asking Brady if he'd lost his mind."

Brady felt his mouth open in surprise. "*Me?* What are you talking about?"

"Cal Grimes is what I'm talking about. My assistant. Well, he used to be until a month ago. He's still got a desk and comes in once a week to help my new assistant get acclimated." Stephen paused. "And on that desk there is now a framed photo of you in uniform."

Ken laughed as Brady covered his face with his hands and groaned, "Kill me now."

"Why thank God?" Wyatt asked before shoving a piece of roast in his mouth.

"He was always very ambitious. A few months ago he started to express his dissatisfaction and last month we agreed he'd outgrown his current position."

Tasha smirked. "Let me translate for the senator. Cal went crazy. Not only did he start doing opposition research for other people and spend his free time elbow-rubbing the kind of lobbyists and politicians Stephen usually avoids, but he started acting so strangely, I thought he might be on drugs. Stephen quietly asked for his resignation and the man actually laughed."

"No comment," Stephen said, ruining his faux-severity by winking at his wife. "Anyway, now I feel bad if his behavior is connected to this sting of Tanaka's.

Is it another federal case?"

"No," Ken answered. "And don't feel bad. If you wanted a second opinion, all I can tell you is that I agree. He's crazy."

"I see." Stephen lowered his brows in concern. "If my office can do anything to help, you know I'm in. I have some experience."

Tasha leaned over to kiss her husband. "One undercover operation and you're going to milk it for the rest of our lives, aren't you, 007?"

"With the bad guy behind bars and the girl in my arms? Damn right."

Jen nudged Brady and gestured toward the salt, then looked across the table at Seamus. "Not to change the subject, especially one that interesting, but I thought Jeremy and Owen would be here."

Seamus looked surprised. "You didn't get the text?"

She shook her head.

"I could have sworn I sent everyone a text." He raised his voice to include the rest of the table. "Did *anyone* get my message about Owen and Jeremy?"

Tasha waggled her fingers. "I didn't get a message from *you*, but Jeremy managed to send me a funny video of Owen at the airport demanding that he turn off his phone and stop texting me. I haven't heard from him since so I guessed they went on vacation. Was I right?"

Everyone at the table turned to Seamus, whose quick glance toward the living room made it clear he felt like swearing. "I was sure I sent a text. And Tasha's right. They left a few days ago. Owen said they'd be gone for two weeks and to tell everyone not to worry if they couldn't get ahold of them."

Brady shared a look with Ken. That must have been the romantic idea Owen had had when he'd purchased plane tickets instead of pizza. "Good for them," he said.

Was Owen actually going to propose? He hoped so. Jeremy was truly one of the good ones.

Seamus snorted at Brady, obviously thinking along the same lines. "Let's just hope he doesn't come back blaming you because it all blew up in his face."

Determined not to have his drunken lecture become the focus of a family interrogation, Brady rushed to fill the silence. "I don't see James either. He always seems to work a double on the nights we get together. Why is his boss such a…" he paused, remembering the children. "Jerk?" he finished proudly.

Solomon—James' boss—glared at his younger brother. "He's busy. Police work doesn't leave a lot of time for extracurricular activities. I'm sure you remember what it was like to work for a living. All those criminals to catch."

"Which is why I like fighting fires," Noah chimed in, distracting Solomon from talking about Brady's old job. "Short bursts of daring heroics framed by weeks of childish pranks and drinking."

"Plus, we're the most popular months in this year's calendar." Wyatt toasted him again and Solomon shook his head.

"Settle down boys or I'll send you to the kids' table." He focused on Ken and Brady instantly tensed. "We may be missing a few family members, but I'm glad *you're* here, Tanaka. I don't think I got a chance to tell you how much I appreciated what you did to help the feds catch Burke and get my cousins out of the corner he'd put them in."

There was too much of Solomon the Elder in his brother's tone for Brady to relax, despite the praise.

Ken, too, seemed prepared for an attack. "I'd like to think anyone in my position would have done the same for a friend," he said carefully.

Solomon set down his fork and wiped his mouth with his napkin. "You do a lot for your friends. Make scandalous pictures disappear as if they never existed, give someone a roof and a job exactly when they need it. Stephen tells me you've even sent his old friend Trick one or two clients in the last few months."

Brady hadn't missed Jen's quiet inhalation at the mention of Trick's name. Damn it. He was definitely going to have a talk with Dunham.

Ken shrugged. "He was the right man for it, and Stephen trusts him. I didn't see any reason not to."

Solomon didn't react. "I suppose I'm wondering why a self-confessed hacker—even one who does freelance work for the feds—would take such a benevolent interest in this family."

The table was silent. Stephen put his hand on Solomon's arm, giving him a look of disapproval, but Brady knew his brother wouldn't respond. He was too busy staring Ken down. Daring him to react.

Brady beat him to it. "I suppose *I'm* wondering why my big brother is acting like such a prick at the dinner table. Can anyone explain it? I know we didn't learn the finer points of table manners from Sol, but I think I still remember his favorite rule—shut up and eat. Why don't we do that?"

Rory chuckled, but Ken's hand gripped Brady's thigh

under the table and squeezed gently, either to hold him back or as a show of gratitude. Brady wasn't sure which, but he responded to the touch instantly and held his tongue.

"I completely understand your concern, Chief Finn. One thing about this family that's always consistent is how protective you are of each other. I admire that."

Ken waited until Solomon nodded in acknowledgment before continuing, "I also admire the proficient officer who accessed my personal records and ran my fingerprints from a terminal in your police station four days ago. Since you know what he found, I'm not sure what else you would need to ease your mind."

Ken hadn't said a word about Solomon's intrusions, but knowing his overprotective brother, Brady wasn't surprised. "Solomon, you're an assh—"

"How the hell could you know who looked what up and *where* they did it?" Solomon asked as if Brady hadn't spoken.

Ken shrugged. "Your precinct's computers are secure and virus free, if that's what you're wondering. I'm alerted anytime someone searches my information. It's a simple program that gives me the time and location of the search. I could help you incorporate it into your systems, if you'd like."

"*I like*," Rory crooned. "Actually I might be in love with you, Tanaka. No one surprises Solomon. It doesn't happen. You're officially my new hero."

Brady glared at Rory, covering Ken's hand possessively with his own. No one could see it, but it made him feel better. His oversexed brother wasn't getting his hands on Ken without going through him. "You obviously didn't find anything too damning, Younger, otherwise you wouldn't have let him inside the house."

Solomon frowned. "You know I hate that nickname. And what I found didn't ease my mind. It was confusing as hell."

"How so?" Ken asked, his serene mask firmly in place.

"You're rich."

"Money confuses you?"

"Cops are so prejudiced," Wyatt muttered to Noah.

Noah nodded. "Damn the man."

"Shut it," Solomon snarled. "I'm not talking to you two. I'm saying he doesn't have to do what he does, which makes me question his reas—"

"You're saying the man you had pegged as a criminal hacker doing probationary work for the feds is actually a wealthy independent contractor who doesn't hesitate to help out a friend in need." Brady finished with grim satisfaction. "He's a good guy with no hidden agenda and you can't let it go because you hate being wrong."

"War made him wise," Noah offered solemnly.

Wyatt swallowed his food with a nod. "The giant redhead speaks sense."

"Shut up," Brady and Solomon said in unison as they glared at Noah and Wyatt.

Tasha started laughing quietly. It was contagious, but Brady held out, still a little ticked at his brother.

Brady knew what Solomon's search had discovered because Ken had already told him most of it. Whatever wasn't classified. He'd been studying computer science and engineering in college, living easily off his trust fund, when curiosity and a little boredom led him into the profession he now quietly dominated.

It started out as harmless snooping, a way to challenge himself. He'd been hacking of course, but never with malicious intent. Just poking his head in to see how far he could get. He got a little too far and discovered some disturbing vulnerabilities in network security programs that were supposed to protect "sensitive" and highly guarded servers.

Ken had been unnerved by the holes he'd found, so he'd started creating programs—new protocols and patches—to fix them. After several visits and lengthy interrogations from men in suits to determine he wasn't a threat, more than one government agency wanted to recruit him full time.

Ken had declined, but offered another solution that made everyone happy. Now the Pentagon and some of the private security contractors on their approved list used his robust, adaptive security software and paid him more than two men could spend in a lifetime for exclusivity.

He also worked for them on occasion, consulting on cyberterrorism cases as well as offering creative surveillance solutions. He enjoyed it, but he never gave up his status as a freelancer. He enjoyed his anonymity more, and having the freedom to help out friends if the need arose, without having to ask for permission.

Ken really was Batman. And Brady was definitely developing a fetish.

Tasha finally caught her breath. "Solomon? You still need to apologize. We were having a great Finn Again until you forgot you weren't at the precinct and started interrogating our dinner guest. Ken's practically one of the family."

"I'm sorry, Tanaka." Solomon muttered.

"It's okay," Ken assured him. "I don't play by ordinary rules, and I know it. When I was at it full time, I'll admit I got results by doing things that would have sent people without my connections to prison."

Ken paused, then fixed his dark golden gaze on Solomon. "Speaking of connections, you may get a phone call."

Solomon shifted in his seat uncomfortably, scowling back at Ken. "Already did. That's why I had to ask." His frown deepened. "So, not full time anymore?"

"I haven't been for years." Ken shrugged. "You said it before. I'm comfortable enough that I don't have to work. I do the odd favor here and there, but if it eases your mind, after this one I'm planning on taking a long, relaxing break."

"Why would it ease his mind?" Wyatt asked, confused.

"Because Solomon's observant," Seamus stated, drawing everyone's attention again. "Really rude, but observant. And Ken—quite the genius himself—

136

understands what he's really asking, so he's assuring your brother that he isn't dangerous. That he's not going to put *anyone* in this family in harm's way. Even if they're working together."

"Oh." Rory looked at Ken closely, then sent a sly smile in Brady's direction. "Oh, I think I get it now. *Good job*, Gigantor."

Oh hell. There was no way anyone knew about—

"I don't," Wyatt groused. "Anyone want to fill the rest of us in?"

"'The rest of us' is shrinking fast, brother mine. Catch up." Noah grinned at Brady. "You big old blue-ox *dog*."

Heat climbed up his neck and he glared. Rory knew. Noah knew. And so did Solomon. Was that why he was being such a jackass to Ken? Was that his twisted way of asking about Tanaka's intentions?

Seamus obviously thought so.

"Seriously, someone tell Wyatt," Rory demanded with a grin. "He hates always being the last to know. I would, but I'm too sadistic."

Jen, who'd been so quiet Brady almost forgot she was there, was the one who volunteered. "Ken and Brady are having sex, Wyatt. With each other. Do I have to explain what goes where, or do they cover that in the firefighter's manual?"

"You are such a *brat*," Wyatt praised, smiling.

She stuck her tongue out at him. "Thank you. It's a defense mechanism to deal with being the only female Finn who isn't five years old and didn't marry into the family. The only one who's usually on the receiving end of all that overprotective, nosy...*love*."

"That's my Little Finn. You tell him," Tasha laughed.

With that, everyone started talking at once, except for Ken. He was looking at Brady. "My turn to ask. Sorry we came?"

Brady hesitated. Was he? He was embarrassed, sure, and still pissed at Solomon. But he wasn't sorry. He was the opposite of sorry. He *wanted* his family to know that Ken was his. Wanted everyone to know that Tanaka was claimed.

Adrenaline made his hand tremble as he moved it to Ken's thigh and dug his fingers into the lean muscle.

"Not sorry," he managed. "But we can't stay."

Ken's gaze heated as he recognized Brady's expression. "I'm not hungry anyway."

"I am."

CHAPTER SEVEN

"Slow down, Brady." Ken's voice had that edge he loved. Need and excitement. Desire. "You don't want to get us pulled over."

Brady smiled and glanced at Ken's pants. He'd worn khaki for dinner and it did nothing to hide the damp spot from his arousal. His body was so fucking responsive. So ready to come.

Some day when he had more control, he'd see if he could make it happen twice in one go.

"I used to pull people over around here during my short career as an officer of the law," he confessed. "It didn't make me a lot of friends, but I know where the speed traps are."

Ken laughed breathlessly his hands gripping either

side of his seat. "I bet you scared the hell out of everyone. A giant unfolding out of his cop car. Sunglasses shielding your eyes. Looking so stern and badass."

"You wouldn't have been scared." Ken wasn't afraid of much.

"You're right. I would have tried to flirt my way into another ticket so I could spend more time imagining you, me and handcuffs. I would have done something to make you frisk me."

The idea didn't make Brady cringe at all. It made him hard. Painfully hard. He glanced up at the freeway exit and hit his blinker, crossing two lanes to get onto the feeder.

"Brady, that's not our exit."

"I know."

There was a place nearby. It must still be there.

Driving with one hand, Brady reached across Ken's body with the other to open the glove compartment. He moved some papers out of the way and hit the jackpot—a flashlight. That would do.

"What's going on? Is something wrong with the car?"

Brady turned onto the dark, vacant cul-de-sac and

sighed in relief. Still here. He used to come here for lunch and to do paperwork. It had always been his place. He'd never told his brothers about it. The last thing he'd wanted was Solomon or James showing up in another squad car to chat. After so many years he couldn't believe that nothing had changed. But he was damn glad it hadn't at the moment.

He put the car in park, letting the engine idle. "Stay there, Tanaka. Don't move."

He got out and wished a little absently for a sedan as he walked around the car's small hood. It didn't matter. It would still work and he would still get what he wanted. What he had to have.

He turned on the flashlight and used it to tap on the window. "Excuse me, sir."

Ken frowned and rolled down the window. "I didn't hear a pop. Do we have a flat tire?"

Brady skimmed the light over his face, watching his pupils contract in reaction. Damn, the man had beautiful eyes. "I need you to step out of your vehicle, sir."

Ken's expression changed from concern to surprised pleasure the moment he realized Brady was playing a part. "Oh. Yes, Officer."

The words got Brady hotter than he'd imagined.

Harder. It made him wish he still had his uniform and everything that came with it. A few minutes ago all he'd wanted was to get inside Ken again. To race for the satisfaction he always found there. Now he wanted to draw it out. To please his lover. To give them both what they wanted.

Ken opened the door and climbed out, holding his arms out to his sides. "What seems to be the trouble?"

Brady pointed the flashlight in the direction he wanted Ken to go. "We'll get to that in a minute. First I want you to face the car and put your hands on the hood. You look like the kind of guy that knows this drill, so don't give me any lip. Just assume the position."

Ken licked the lips in question, his steps steady and careful as he did as Brady asked. "I think you've pulled over the wrong man, Officer. I'm a law-abiding citizen. I've never been stopped or ticketed in my life."

Brady moved until he was right behind him and put one hand on his hip, using his feet to nudge Ken's farther apart. "That's what they all say," he said in a brusque, authoritative voice. "Sir, do you have anything on your person that you'd like to tell me about? Anything you're concealing that could be construed as dangerous and/or illegal? This will go easier for you if you tell me now."

Brady heard Ken's breathing catch, saw the cheeks of his ass flex beneath the khaki fabric. "No sir, Officer. Nothing. I've got nothing to hide."

"We'll see about that." Brady held the small flashlight in his mouth and started to frisk Ken. The first pass was by the book, patting down his legs, arms and waistline. He found Ken's thin wallet with his identification in one pocket, pulled it out and tossed it on the hood. In the other, he found a small travel-sized bottle of lube.

He smiled around the metal. Leave it to Tanaka to be this prepared.

Taking the flashlight out of his mouth, he set it and the bottle on the hood beside Ken's hands. "Look what I found without even trying. If I take a closer look, am I going to come across anything else? Something you don't want me to see?"

"N-no. No, that's all. I'm not hiding anything else."

He bit back a moan when he pressed his erection against Ken's back. He felt a shudder rack that lean frame and closed his eyes, counting. "I want to believe you, sir, but I wouldn't be good at my job if I didn't take my time and make sure."

"Fuck," Ken whispered, making Brady smile.

"Don't move," he ordered. "Keep your hands on the vehicle."

"Yes, Officer."

"If I had my cuffs I could make sure of it, but I'll have to take your word." God, he really wished he had those cuffs.

"My belt would work," Ken offered weakly.

He didn't like kink, Brady reminded himself even as he eyed the belt hungrily. He wasn't into bondage. All he wanted was to drive Ken crazy before he fucked him. "Don't give me ideas."

He yanked Ken's shirt up and lifted until it went over his head and down his arms. "Tattoos. You know what kind of man gets his back covered in tattoos?"

Ken shivered. "Someone who likes tattoos, sir?"

He yelped when Brady's hand popped his ass. "Some people like tattoos, yes. But no one likes a smartass. I think a man with this much pretty ink on his back wants to spend a lot of time bent over by his lover."

He leaned closer and kissed Ken's shoulder tenderly, his touch at odds with his tone. "Do you like being bent over?"

"Yes," Ken moaned. "Oh, yes."

He reached around him and clumsily undid the narrow strip of fabric Ken had belted around his pants. He laid it down between Ken's hands, away from him so he wouldn't be tempted to use it. "Let's take a look at what else you're hiding without that in our way."

He unbuttoned Ken's pants, lowering the zipper before taking a step back and yanking the fabric roughly down his thighs. "What do we have here?"

The tightest, hottest ass I've ever seen, Brady groaned silently. No matter how many times he'd been inside it, it was never enough. "Lube and no underwear. No wonder you were in such a hurry. I was right. Someone was on his way to get lucky."

"Yes," Ken moaned. "I have a date. He'll be worried if I don't show up soon. If you'll just give me a ticket…"

Fuck, he was playing his role just right. Brady's adrenaline was through the roof, and he couldn't take his eyes off Ken's ass. He reached out and cupped it with his palm, caressing the firm cheeks. "You want a ticket? Well, I want to know what you're hiding in here."

His thumbs spread Ken's ass cheeks apart, letting the night air hit that small ring of muscles that tempted him. "I bet your date knows, doesn't he? What's inside? I bet he gets himself off just thinking about it when you're not around. Thinking about how tight you are. Thinking about how loud you scream, how sweetly you grip him when you come with his dick buried inside you."

"Bra—Officer, *please*."

Brady took a hand away from Ken's ass and placed it between his shoulder blades. "I want you flat, hands stretched over your head."

He gently pressed and Ken resisted. "Why?"

Brady growled, increasing the pressure until Ken obeyed. "Because I said so and you don't want me to take you in." He moved Ken until his ass was tilted up toward him, only the toes of his shoes touching the ground. "Because I'm not done searching this body and I'm nothing if not fucking thorough."

He spread Ken's cheeks wide and lowered his head, licking the seam of his lover's ass before stiffening his tongue to push inside. *Yes. Oh, yeah.* He'd wanted to do this for days.

"Oh God." Ken's moan was muffled by Brady's racing heart. "Your tongue... Fuck it's good. Fuck..."

So good. He was tongue-fucking Ken's ass like a man possessed. Starved. He'd bent his lover over against his car in a public place and he couldn't stop. Couldn't care. Anyone could see them. Anyone watching might think that Brady actually was a dirty, kinky cop who pulled sexy men over to have his way with them. To shove his tongue deep inside their tight asses and make them want more. Make them beg for his cock.

God, he was twisted, but the fantasy was too good. And Ken was loving it. All of it. And there was nothing he could imagine that wouldn't turn him on as long as he was doing it with Tanaka.

Brady lifted his mouth and gasped for air. "I've got the right man, don't I? I know you have what I'm looking for. What I want."

Ken put his shaking hands behind his back, his fingers clasped together. "I won't make it easy. I won't tell you where it is. You can just keep looking until you find it. You'll never take me in."

Brady smiled with a clenched jaw as he reached for the lube. "The only place I'm taking you now is on the hood of this car. I'm going to go so deep I'll know all your secrets. And there is *nothing* you can do about it."

"Yes, Officer. You're in charge. I can't do anything to stop you." Ken sounded desperate. *Aroused.* Jesus, he was so fucking sexy.

"Damn right I'm in charge." He undid his jeans and coated his cock with lube, dripping some between Ken's cheeks. "And you have the right to scream your beautiful head off as I use this against you."

Ken's laugh turned into a howl of pleasure when Brady pushed the head of his shaft into that tight fucking hole. *Oh hell yes.* It had only been a few hours and it might as well have been weeks. He couldn't live without it. Couldn't last a day without that painful squeeze around his cock.

He felt sweat drip down his back and could have sworn it steamed off his skin in reaction to the charge building at the base of his spine. He rocked slowly, filling Ken one inch at a time. Showing him he was in control. He would set the pace, no matter how much it killed him.

"Please," Ken whimpered, letting go of his other hand and reaching back to touch Brady's hip. "So good. Need it... *Please.*"

Brady inhaled sharply as he caught sight of the belt halfway hidden by Ken's body. Dragging it out from beneath damp flesh, he wrapped it around Ken's wrists. "I think you need help following orders."

Ken stilled beneath him, looking back over his shoulder while Brady made sure his wrists were secure and then held both ends of the belt in one hand. Brady was too turned on to decipher the expression in those wide golden eyes.

"Is that good?" he growled, only half in character.

Ken nodded swiftly, biting his lip.

"Good." Brady bent his knees and slung his hips forcefully, filling Ken's ass in one stroke. "*So. Fucking. Good.*"

He gripped Ken's hip with his free hand, holding him steady for each powerful thrust. *Take it, baby. Take all of me. Right here. Anywhere I want. Anytime. Tell me it's mine. Your ass…your mouth. God, it's so good I can't stop. I never will. Never letting go.*

Ken was crying out, muttering his name like a prayer, but Brady couldn't stop. He looked down at his white-knuckled grip on the belt that held Ken's wrists together, and when he saw his thick shaft impaling that greedy ass, he felt like a conqueror. Like a barbarian enjoying his spoils. It was heady, dangerously addictive, and he didn't care.

Mine.

He lost track of time. They were both moaning and drenched in sweat and still he refused to go faster, not wanting it to end. Ken struggled against the belt, but Brady wouldn't give in.

Don't want to stop. So tight. Don't want it to end.

"Brady," Ken shouted. "*Let me come.*"

"Beg me," he rasped.

"Please, Brady. I'm *begging* you to fuck me harder. Faster. I need that thick cock. I need to come. *Please.* I'll do anything."

This time it got through, a panicked thread in Ken's voice that he understood. "You need it that bad? Then come for me, baby. Come with me."

His hips picked up a swift, hard rhythm that had Ken shouting in relief and arousal. "Oh yeah. *Harder.* Don't hold back. Fuck, I'm so close. Brady it's too—"

Brady didn't hold back. He couldn't. His own needs had taken the wheel, racing toward the one destination he knew he needed. When the crash came it exploded around him and he shook with it, his whole body reeling as it spun him into oblivion.

Yes. Perfect.

I wanted this to last.

Ken's cries sent Brady's hand between his body and the car so he could feel the slick proof of his lover's climax.

So responsive, he crooned silently. *So good, baby.*

After he recovered enough, Brady kissed Ken's back

and unwound his belt, helping him to stand. He turned him around and fell to his knees, pausing to clean Ken's wet cock with his tongue. Ken shivered as Brady lingered over the thick head to savor the salty taste of his release. He was still shivering when Brady pulled up his pants and slipped his wallet back into his pocket.

"Are you taking care of me?" Ken asked softly, his lashes lowered over his eyes almost shyly.

"That depends. Do you like it?" Brady stood up and pulled him close, burying his face in the crook of Ken's neck.

Ken leaned into him. "I think so. I'm not used to it, but I think so."

Brady closed his eyes for a moment and sighed. They were one hell of a pair. "Let's get you home."

"That sounds good. Take me home, Officer. It's the least you can do after that thorough cavity search. I'm not sure I could drive."

Lifting his head, Brady smiled down at Ken before reaching for his shirt and slipping it back over his head. "I take my job seriously."

He drove them back to the warehouse in silence. He knew every bend and curve and warp in the road, and Ken's eyes were closed as if he'd fallen asleep, so he let his mind wander.

That was a little more than their usual round of rough sex.

A little?

Okay, it was a hell of a lot more than sex. Brady hadn't felt like himself. He'd done things—tying Ken up with his own belt—that he would never think to do when he was clear-headed.

Maybe he was making too much of it. They'd both been impatient to get home and, on impulse, they'd given in to a harmless fantasy. Sexy cop and the traffic stop with a happy ending.

Only it hadn't felt harmless.

Ken sensed it too. Brady had seen it in his eyes. Had he crossed some kind of invisible kink line? Should he apologize for going too far? For making the decision to pull over without asking first?

He seemed to recall Tasha talking about rules at the club. About being safe, sane and consensual. There were a lot of rules, but those were the easiest to remember. And they sounded normal enough. Everyone wanted that.

But he wasn't sure that they'd been *any* of those in the last few days. He glanced over at Ken and revised his statement. Ken was all about being consensual, no matter what Brady did. He never turned him away and never turned him down. But one out of three still didn't sound like that great a track record.

There was a part of him that wanted to apologize. Even wanted to be ashamed of himself—the way he'd been after he watched Ken shower. But he couldn't bring himself to do it.

It was Ken. It was hot as hell, dirty as fuck, and it was Ken. His body was still recovering from how good it was and he'd be willing to do it again. Nothing with Ken Tanaka felt wrong.

If Brady was guilty of anything, it was of being wrong about what he did and didn't find arousing. There was no way he could have known he had this in him. That he wasn't as vanilla as everyone—including himself—believed. He didn't know he had another flavor. No one had ever made him feel kinky. Well, kinky enough. But Ken did.

What about Ken's kink?

Brady frowned. It hadn't come up. So far everything had been about him, about what he wanted. Was Ken okay with that because he wasn't expecting this to last? Or was he hoping for more give and take? He hadn't said anything, hadn't mentioned anything about it since their fight in the gym.

He needed to stop thinking about this. He didn't want to waste a minute of tonight worrying about rope and kink and whether or not commitment was on Ken's radar.

A lot depended on what happened tomorrow. If everything went according to plan, the day after would be for reunions and celebrations. And the day after that? If Ken gave him a chance, Brady promised himself he would tell him how he felt.

He wasn't backing away again.

CHAPTER EIGHT

Brady did his best to blend into the wall as he waited for Cal Grimes to finish his phone call. The club was so loud he'd had to take it outside, leaving Brady alone as an out-of-place extra in a Rob Zombie movie.

From the outside, the nightclub looked like a nondescript furniture outlet off the highway. An ordinary building, with a few oddly dressed club kids smoking near the entrance. Brady had been imagining an old church on a desolate stretch of road or a private high rise with no escape, but this was a populated area. Maybe it wouldn't be that bad. He'd started to relax until they'd pushed through the large metal doors and the atmosphere had shattered his illusions and punched him right between the eyes.

This is what he imagined Hell looked like. Or at least, one level of it. He was pretty sure it wasn't his age talking. Even Jen would turn around and run home after hearing what they were pretending was music—horrifying screams set to a dance beat. The lights above the crowd were swinging and swirling and pulsing enough to make the strongest stomach queasy, and men and women—most wearing latex, black lipstick, and apathy—shuffled their boneless bodies around the dance floor as if they were undead and this club was where they'd all been confined for everyone else's safety.

Why wasn't he drinking again? A bottle or three of rum sounded like it would hit the spot right now. Brady sighed, taking it all in and knowing this wasn't the worst of it. This was only the facade for the real horror story going on one level up. He doubted any of these Goth groupies even knew it existed. That there was a private club where people who were too rich to be famous gathered and played games with other people's lives.

There was no reason they should know. According to Cal, the elevator was hidden and the only way up was with a special key card. For VIP members, the same elevator allowed access through a separate entrance in a secure garage.

Cal wasn't a VIP yet, but he did possess a card.

Was Ken already up there? He'd left several hours earlier to pick up his play partner and get set up, giving Brady the kind of good luck kiss that made him want to drag his lover back to bed and never leave. Fucking tease.

Brady left the loft shortly afterward, still turned on but grateful to Ken for trying to keep him distracted. He'd spent the whole day describing the club he was a member of—the potlucks and Halloween parties, the laughter and lighthearted demonstrations. Whatever his friends had told him about *this* place made Ken nervous.

Ken didn't get nervous, so Brady was a walking ball of stress. He used his short motorcycle ride to exorcise a few of those demons. He needed to bring his A game tonight. Needed to keep sharp and alert, and above all, to look like he was enjoying himself. This could all go to hell fast if he didn't.

He met Cal in the parking lot of Finn's Pub, a black dress jacket over his t-shirt and jeans. How Ken had managed to purchase something that fit him so well was a mystery, but one that met with Cal's distracted approval.

Right away it was clear something was different. Cal

was wired. Excitement and anticipation were making him restless as the car took them to their location. Underneath that there was something else. Fear? He didn't proposition Brady once, which had to be a first, and he honestly wasn't sure what to make of it. It was strange, being with Grimes without Ken in his ear keeping him sane and telling him what to say. But it wasn't possible tonight. Brady was, for the most part, on his own, and he couldn't fuck it up because he'd made Ken a promise to help bring Terry home.

Almost there, he thought. *Almost done.*

Several of the nightclub's patrons noticed him leaning against the wall and sent him curious looks. When Brady smiled tightly, two of them came closer, staring at his hair with wide eyes.

Brady's smile widened with genuine amusement. Did the color red confuse them?

Cal appeared in front of them and took Brady's hand, glaring until the strange creatures backed away. "Looks like I got back to rescue my prize just in time."

Brady let himself be led, noticing the dampness of Cal's palms. "It's easy to forget they're just kids."

"They're foul demon spawn who have no respect for authority. I've spoken to the other members about either finding an alternate location or closing this lower floor down for good. Let them hate the world in someone's basement."

Someone got teased the first few times he came here, Brady decided.

"That's a little harsh," he said. "They're young. Having no respect for authority is a given when you're young."

"Says the cop-turned-Marine."

Brady shrugged. "I'm a regular civilian now. But a Marine would say that good people fight and die for their right to wear those outfits and hate the world, so who are we to judge?" And now he felt guilty, because he'd definitely been judging.

Cal guided him to the back of the club, past the DJ booth and down a hall. He kept moving beyond the little Goth's room—a unisex restroom with a bored-looking stick figure on a black door—until they came to what looked like a utility closet. Cal swung open the closet door and slipped inside the small room with Brady following close behind.

Cal moved around him, surreptitiously glancing back down the hall before shutting the door behind them.

Brady was bemused. "Are we in stealth mode?"

Cal rolled his eyes. "You can be pious all you like. I don't want those bottom feeders getting too nosy."

He motioned toward an open elevator that seemed out of place on the far wall of the dingy room. As they stepped into the sparkling clean cubicle, Cal took his key card out of his pocket and then stopped to stare at Brady for a long, tense moment. "Sometimes I'm not sure if I'm right about you."

Shit. Brady tilted his head, trying to send Cal one of the sensual smiles Ken used that always worked on him. "What do you mean?"

"You don't have to put on a show like the rest of them. You don't have to pretend to be the perfect moral specimen, like your cousin." Cal's laugh was strained. "I mean, you're not angling for sainthood, are you?"

Brady braced himself and walked purposefully toward Cal, towering over him until he'd backed up against the elevator wall, clutching his key card. "You know me better than that by now, don't you, Cal?"

Cal's lips parted and he started to pant. "I…I thought I did. But I don't know why you didn't tell me you were staying with that man."

Fucking hell. "Tanaka?" He shook his head and laughed, scrambling for a smooth answer. "I'm staying on the floor in an office in his building. It's embarrassing to admit to someone you want to impress."

Cal frowned suspiciously. "He hasn't tried anything? He's a rope Dom with a lot of money to throw around and friends in high places. He never came on to you?"

Brady moved in closer and lowered his voice, knowing how important this was. "If he did, I haven't noticed. He's a friend of Tasha's and she knew he had extra space. So she did me a favor, getting the guy to let me crash at his place when Owen not-so-subtly kicked me out. That's all it is, Cal. You're the only one I'm dating. The one I'm on the phone with every night."

"I know," Cal whispered.

"Either I'm a sinner or a saint, Cal. You decide. If you want me to play saint, I will," he offered smoothly, hating himself. "But I'd rather not with you."

Cal's free hand reached between them, slipping under Brady's shirt to touch his flat stomach. Brady flinched in surprise but Cal closed his eyes and moaned, the hand holding the key card shaking. "I don't want a saint, Brady. I want you to be the big, hard Marine who came back wanting more. Wanting what I can give you. You've kept me waiting and teased me for days. You're bad and I want a bad boy. A big, bad boy that I can take home and punish."

Don't throw up. Keep smiling when you back away. Almost done. "Then we're on the same page."

He moved back until he was leaning against the opposite wall and started his internal countdown to calm himself down. He didn't want this to take more than an hour. Especially now that Cal had brought up Tanaka.

How had he found out?

Cal was more relaxed than he'd been since he picked Brady up. He smiled and inserted the key card, pushing a few buttons on a keypad before the doors closed and their short ascent began. Brady pretended he didn't notice.

"I knew you'd come around, Brady. Knew you were different. When you told me you were interested in exploring your darker urges, it took a lot of restraint on my part not to bring you here right away. But you weren't ready. You needed to know me. To feel safe with me. Even trust me. I think that's happened, hasn't it?"

No.

"Definitely," he said instead.

"That's why, when I found out your roommate was crashing the party, I made sure it was canceled. I don't want anything distracting us, or anyone reporting back to the senator's wife. After tonight, things will be different between us," Cal promised, obviously unaware that he'd thrown Brady a surprise punch in the solar plexus. "It might shock you at first, what you see here. The senator's wife thinks she knows what kink is, but she has no idea. Try to keep an open mind. If you can do that for me, I'll make sure you won't regret it. And when you meet my friends, you'll finally understand what I can give to you. What being with me will do for everyone you care about. Your family."

Brady's shoulders tensed and he forced himself not to throw Cal against the wall for mentioning his family. "And here I thought it was just a party with some kinky toys."

"It's so much more than that, Brady. It changed my life." The elevator stopped and the doors opened, but Cal stopped him with a hand on his chest. "Before you take another step, you need to know that you can never talk to anyone but me about what you see here. My friends are serious about their privacy. They'll do anything to ensure it."

Brady made himself smile and relaxed his posture, still feeling like a heel for leading him on. "Of course,

Cal."

"Stay close to me. Don't wander off by yourself and don't talk to anyone unless they speak directly to you first."

Brady had no desire to talk to anyone but Vargas, so he let Cal's strict instructions slide. He would behave until he could get close enough to shake his hand. That was all that needed to happen. Ken's program would do the rest.

At least it was quieter up here. If you ignored the sound of floggers and the blood-curdling screams of pain. He followed Cal and took in the large space as he went, making note of all the possible exits out of habit. The place was surprisingly utilitarian—the walls were gray with black trim, the furniture was red and the lights were bright and unflattering. No one cared about aesthetics or ambiance, that was clear. The only decorations were living and begging for mercy.

He instinctively looked for Ken—his long black braid and wicked smile, his tattooed back and beautiful body. But each time his gaze collided with a scene that made him queasy, he was glad he wasn't there. Brady had seen a lot of gruesome things in his years of combat, but some of this was just plain wrong.

The first was a naked man whose arms were spread wide on a cross and held in place by thick metal chain. His knees were bent, his feet resting on a small protrusion on the device, and his entire body was covered in bloody welts. Brady assumed those came from the man wielding a multi-tailed whip that was tipped with sharp metal edges. Brady flinched when he looked down and noticed the clothespins attached to his testicles.

Son of—*God* that looked painful. Truly. And the man genuinely looked miserable. As if he would stand and try to leave if there weren't fucking mousetraps on the floor to keep him from lowering his feet.

Had he voluntarily asked for this? *Why?*

Open mind, Brady. Remember your training and tighten up. Stick to the mission.

He tried. He passed another man hanging from metal hooks inserted into his back. The Conan-wannabe behind him whipped his ass ferociously and ordered him not to move, which was impossible because the force of the blows made the hanging man rock forward. He was helpless and dangling with no way to obey. No way to get down.

Brady clenched his fists at his sides, then quickly

opened them and hooked his thumbs in his pockets so no one would notice his tension. *Open mind, my ass.* He wanted to break that damn whip and cut that poor guy down. He'd reached his limit as soon as he got off the elevator. Only fifty-five minutes to go.

Did Ken like things like this? Did he *do* things like this? He couldn't see it. Couldn't merge these images with the man who was his lover.

He thought about the night Ken had bound Tasha. Brady knew it was just a demo, and it had all been for show, but it hadn't looked anything like this. Ken had moved like he was dancing, and his hands had been commanding but soothing. Everything about him that night had been focused on his partner, on her pleasure. This? This was all about pain without mercy. This was everything he'd thought BDSM was when he first met Ken. Torture. Humiliation. Power.

Were any of these men Terry Wahl? If not, had *they* been tricked, trapped and traded into being sex slaves, as he had? Most of the men who weren't being tortured were chained to the wall—waiting for their turn to be abused by the ones wielding the whips, chains and knives. Did they want to be here? Were they given an option?

He glanced over his shoulder and took a closer look at the wrestlers dressed as security guards stationed throughout the room. There were telltale bulges under their shirts. Armed wrestlers. Even better.

How was he going to do this without Ken?

Just do it, that's how. Focus.

Cal squeezed his hand. "My friends are at that viewing table up there." Brady noticed a few carpeted steps leading to a row of tables, one of them occupied. "Don't worry, I have no intention of talking shop tonight, but I need to say hello. I want to show you off."

Yes, finally. The reason he was here.

"I don't mind," Brady said, speaking through the knot of disgust in his throat. "I'd like to meet them. And if you want to talk for a while? We're not in any hurry, right?"

Cal frowned. "You might not be, but I damn well am."

As they slowly climbed the steps, Brady observed the four men he was going to meet. Their ages ranged from forties to sixty-something and their clothing was casual, but expensively so. He memorized their individual features, but it wasn't easy since they all had a similar look about them. That look was money. So much money they didn't need to count it or talk about it. So much that they didn't understand what a budget was and never heard the word "no." Only one of them was looking down toward the main floor. The rest were having a quiet discussion, showing little to no interest in the painful scenes of torture they'd supposedly come to see. From their expressions, they could have been at their yacht club or playing golf instead of watching naked men bleed.

These were the kind of men Cal Grimes admired. This Slaver's Club. These were the kind of men he wanted to emulate. But it was clear none of the men at the table were self-made. None of them had an air of ambition or drive. They had more in common with the apathy-filled club kids downstairs. The fact that they'd seen this sort of sexual brutality enough for it to bore them made Brady want to break something off in their asses. Something sharp and painful. But they'd probably get off on that, the lecherous fucks.

Brady didn't want to know men like these. He didn't want to shake their hands and pretend he enjoyed meeting them. He just needed one man for one minute.

Unfortunately, that man wasn't at the table. Ken had shown him the only picture he'd found of the financier so Brady would recognize him. He was heavyset with a beard and a receding hairline. He was in town, and he should be here. He was supposed to be here.

Brady calmed his panic and focused on the others. They were deep in discussion about something that obviously upset the younger man. His posture was defensive, his expression volatile. But nothing he said made the others react in kind. Brady tried to guess what it could be about. A merger gone wrong? A country they wouldn't let him buy? Or did the little evil Cabal member want a pony?

Before Brady could come close enough to hear anything interesting, they stopped talking and started to turn in his direction.

They've seen you. No backing out now, Finn.

"Good lord, Grimes wasn't exaggerating was he, boys? That has to be a first." The man closest to the stairs chuckled, his expression surprised as he looked Brady up and down without leaving his chair. "He's bigger than my head of security, and that man is a mutant."

The younger member, Pony Boy, stood and moved closer in silence. He shook hands with Grimes, but the entire time he was studying the zipper of Brady's jeans as if he could lower it by will alone.

"Did you say he was a Marine, as well?"

"Yes," Cal answered proudly, as if he'd enlisted himself. "He was commended more than once for heroism and valor in combat."

"It's nice to meet you," Brady forced out stiffly, wishing he'd been sent here to knock some heads together instead of playing Cal's date. "Thank you for letting me—"

"He has a nice voice, too," the third man interrupted, reminding Brady that Cal had told him not to speak unless spoken to. "Very deep. Very commanding."

Brady felt drunk again. He was nauseated and not quite sure any of this was really happening. In fact, it was so much like a bad movie he had to swallow a laugh.

"Well done for your first time out, Grimes. To be honest, I didn't think you'd get him here voluntarily. But looking at him now, I can see why you went to so much trouble. If he weren't so well connected, he would be a perfect addition to our stables."

Addition to your what, *motherfucker?* Brady looked down at Cal who was wisely avoiding eye contact. Brady no longer felt sorry for stringing him along. He no longer felt anything but quiet, seething rage.

Stay on mission. Smile. Relax. Imagine what you'd do to them if you could. That should cheer you up.

"The senator only has pull in this state," Cal protested. "We have other clubs."

Pony Boy frowned at Cal. "*We* have other clubs. You've only been invited to this one, so take care. And you're still an idiot. The senator has more influence and political capital than he did before. And this big bruiser was there. He knows what happened." He laughed. "You can't handle a ride like this, Grimes. He would break you."

Cal's face turned red. "He's mine. He wants to be here. Tell them, Brady."

"I want to be here." *To burn your house down.* Brady smiled genially.

All four men laughed at that and Pony Boy patted Cal on the shoulder. "I can see he's overcome with lust." He paused. "Are you sure you wouldn't consider sharing him? I've been disappointed once already this evening. In fact, we could make the argument that you were personally responsible for that, so you owe me."

Cal took a step forward. "I don't care. I'm not sharing him."

No one is sharing me you sick, nasty jackoffs. Brady nodded in agreement with Cal, showing the men his pleased expression. *Try it and you'll lose a limb.*

Pony Boy didn't look happy with that answer, but his tone was amused. "For now, that might be best. You're our newest member, definitely our first charity case, and you've been here more than the rest of us combined these last two weeks. You need your own toy so you don't break all of ours."

Cal seemed confused. As if he didn't know whether or not he'd been insulted.

Oh you have, buddy. Trust me. He doesn't like you at all.

None of them did. It was obvious to Brady, but confusing. It wasn't like they were low on whipping boys. Why had they let Cal join if they couldn't stand him?

The fourth man set down his drink. "Look at what he was working for, Clive. That is a prime piece of real estate. The size of him alone gives one ideas. Any of us would have used the club's amenities as roughly in the same situation. Once Vargas is finished with Cal's favorite piece of equipment, he'll see this strapping Marine and say the same. He'll probably try to purchase him from you, Grimes, but don't you let him."

Cal frowned. "He's… I didn't know he liked that one."

Clive/Pony Boy snorted and shared a laughing look with the others. "He doesn't, really. He has his own toys. He's just not that fond of you. He'll come around to our way of thinking. You've already been invaluable."

Brady knew he could turn around and walk out. There was no doubt in his mind that none of the guards, armed or not, could stop him. Not if they wanted to remain intact. One word stopped him.

Vargas.

He has his own toys.

Ken wasn't here. Brady was the only one who could salvage this shitstorm and finish the mission. He turned and looked down at Cal, raising his eyebrows expectantly and hoping his anger would come off as excitement instead. "Your favorite? That sounds promising."

"Show him, Cal," one of the men urged. "His reaction should be interesting. They're in the back room."

Cal hesitated, trying to read Brady's expression. "You remember what I told you about keeping an open mind?"

Nodding as nonchalantly as he could, Brady used Ken's trademark smile so he wouldn't have to speak.

Cal's shoulders relaxed. "Good. Come with me."

Brady shoved his hands deep into his jean pockets so Cal wouldn't take his hand. If he did Brady might break his bones. Slowly. One at a time. And then he might reset them and do it again.

Burke was a blackmailer who liked kink. These men were something else entirely. Brady wanted to laugh them off as stereotypical spoiled pricks but... *They didn't care.* They didn't care that Brady had been listening to them while they talked about his cousin. They didn't care that he knew what they looked like or where this club was located. That wasn't stupidity, and it wasn't coming off as blatant overconfidence. It was knowledge.

That made them dangerous.

"I told you on our first date that everyone would want to take you home. Clive already does."

Cal said it like Brady was supposed to be pleased. What happened to the man? He'd been Stephen's assistant, for crying out loud. How could he think this was okay? That this was acceptable behavior? "How did you meet your friends?"

"They found me nearly three months ago," Cal told him. "But they'd had their eye on me for a while. They said I had exactly the kind of ambition they were looking for, and that was more important than my pedigree." He sounded so proud. "I'm the first man to gain membership without generations of money behind me. Do you know how impossible that is? And since then I've had more work than I know what to do with, more money than I've ever made and this. All of this, whenever I want it. Everything is finally working for me. That's why I knew I could have you too. When you know these men, nothing is impossible."

Aw, hell, the stupid bastard was a fall guy. Brady didn't have proof, and he didn't know when they would throw him to the wolves, but he knew it would happen. Greed and lust did strange things to people, and Cal had an overabundance of both. The men here would know exactly how to exploit it.

Brady might feel sorry for him if Cal hadn't just paraded him in front of those men like a prize bull. It had been the worst sort of humiliation. Not purposeful, just matter-of-fact. They spoke about him, not at him, enumerating his traits and studying the goods for future reference.

He'd been an object. A thing. He wondered if they'd still feel that way if he took turns dangling them out a window by their ankles.

Focus. For Ken. For Terry. You made a promise.

"They didn't treat you very well." *Damn it, Brady, shut up.* "I mean, you deserve better."

Cal stopped walking and whirled to face Brady, his hand coming up as if he thought he could slap him. Instinctively, Brady's own hand shot up to grip Cal's wrist lightly. Just enough pressure to stop him, and then he let him go.

"You say another word about them and I will get the guards to hold you down while I beat you." Cal was whispering, quick and panicked. "I want you but I will be damned if I let you ruin this for me. They chose me. *Me.* Clive is jealous, because he's not the young hotshot anymore. I am. This is what I deserve."

Fix this. Tighten up. "I'm sorry, Cal. I shouldn't have said anything."

"That's right," he said, straightening his jacket. "Now I really need that ride so I don't hurt you later. I hope Vargas is done."

The back room wasn't that different from the rest of

this sadistic nightmare, but it had a wall for privacy. There was also what looked like a medical curtain, behind which Brady could see a heavyset, bearded shadow, pumping away.

Almost done.

That was Vargas. It had to be.

Cal swore under his breath when he saw the shadow and took a step closer, his hands folded tightly together. He waited until Vargas had taken a breath between grunts and called out, "Are you almost done with him?"

"I'll be out when I'm finished," Vargas groaned. "I'm showing him how it's done."

Him. *Sonofbitchmotherfuc*— They'd been talking about a person, Brady realized. Not a machine or accessory. Vargas was using Cal's favorite *person.*

Brady was genuinely concerned he might be sick. He grimaced in disgust, using the opportunity to look for his target's clothes. *One break*, he prayed. *One break and I can get the hell out of here and find Ken.*

There. Vargas' jacket was neatly folded on a chair in the corner. His phone was right on top. *There is a God.* Brady walked around the scene, pretending fascination with different implements on the table beside the chair. He angled his body until the jacket and phone were behind him.

Almost there.

Vargas was grunting on top of that poor son of a bitch and Cal couldn't seem to decide if he was upset or aroused as he moved a little closer and looked around the curtain.

It was now or never. While Cal was absorbed with getting his "turn", Brady stepped back until he felt the fabric of the jacket brush his jeans, slipped his hand into his pocket and turned his small phone on. It vibrated once, confirming it was working.

One minute. That's how long Ken told him it would take to clone the phone. Every name and phone number, every account and every message Vargas got would be theirs. Most importantly, so would his GPS.

One minute was too long, Brady thought, keeping count.

As he waited, he came to a realization. Whether things worked out with Ken or not, this was his next job. Stopping this. Making these men suffer and lose everything they thought protected them from punishment. Stopping this.

There was no reality where they would get away.

One minute. The phone buzzed silently in his pocket,

two quick pulses to let him know it was done.

Finally.

Vargas finished with a gasping, "I think he likes me better, Grimes. But you can have a turn now if you want."

Cal was already slipping off his jacket and unbuttoning his pants when Brady put a hand on his shoulder. "Cal?"

Cal's cheeks were flushed when he sent Brady a pleading smile. "Would you be too jealous, Brady? You're the only man I want. I just started playing because you made me wait." He lowered his voice. "Now I sort of have to do this or he'll think he's won."

Grimes would look so much better with a broken nose.

Get out. Say anything. "Oh yeah, I get it. But I have to take a piss so I was hoping you could start without me. Just don't finish until I'm back. I'd like to see that."

Cal nodded, relief and arousal making him amenable. "I want you to see it, so you'll have to hurry. I promise it'll be your turn as soon as I'm done. Restrooms are to the right of the elevator, next to the kitchen. Don't wander—just come right back here when you're done or Clive might try to steal you."

Brady smiled and nodded, then turned and walked away without another word, his mind racing to find a way down that elevator to freedom. He was thinking he could trick one of the guards into the bathroom, knock him out and take his key card. It would have to be quiet and quick, and there'd be no room for mistakes, but it wasn't anything he hadn't done before.

It would be easier than staying in this club.

He frowned when he got to the elevator. The guards weren't there. He walked toward the restrooms to buy more time, his gaze skimming the bare walls. Where were those damned armed wrestlers when he needed them?

Brady pushed open the door and found himself flat on his face with a knee in his back before he could react or make a sound.

"Brady?"

The knee disappeared and Ken was there, rolling him over and smiling with those perfect lips. "Are you ready to go yet?"

He stifled his wildly inappropriate laughter as relief temporarily replaced his rage. Ken was there, in a black t-shirt and black pants, ready to save the day. "You'll never know how ready. I cloned the phone but we need a key card."

"We don't, but pick one if you'd like a souvenir." Ken pointed toward the bathroom stalls and Brady saw five mostly unconscious guards tied up and gagged on the floor, their empty guns and keycards beside them.

"Damn it, Tanaka. I was really looking forward to hitting someone and you had to show off like a damn ninja. How did you get up here? I know Cal canceled your demo."

Ken's expression was feral. "Is he the one? I'll have to thank him for that." He smiled at Brady. "I wasn't going to let you have all the fun, Finn. After the call, I came anyway, bypassed the elevator lock and started rounding up these losers. I figured you'd want to leave as soon as possible."

Brady grabbed Ken and kissed him, nearly lifting him off his feet in the process. When he pulled back Ken's eyes were worried. "That bad, huh?"

"I can't talk about it now. We need to leave before Grimes finishes up and comes looking for me. Before Pony Boy sees us."

"Pony Boy? Let them come. I mean it." The look in Ken's golden eyes was deadly. "From what little I've seen since I got here? I could take them."

He motioned confidently toward the pile of disarmed men and Brady was tempted—but something felt off. They bastards hadn't noticed that all their guards were missing. This wasn't that big of a place and it wasn't that crowded, yet no one had sounded an alarm. Just more overconfidence…or something more sinister? "Later."

They left the restroom together, walking casually toward the elevator. Brady kept a lookout while Ken punched in the code to open the doors. He heard the whoosh and turned, ready to breathe a sigh of relief, when he saw the guard inside.

Without thinking, Brady rushed him, gripped him in a chokehold and cut off his air before he could cry for help. Ken joined him, punched in another code and sent the elevator down. As the doors closed, Brady slammed the guard's head against the wall just hard enough to give him a headache when he finally regained consciousness.

"You missed one."

"I was saving him for you."

CHAPTER NINE

Would he ever feel completely clean again?

Brady sighed as he felt the water begin to cool. By the time they'd made it home, he was one raw nerve saturated in adrenaline. He'd handed the clone phone to Ken the minute they got outside the club and smashed his own cell against the wall, throwing the pieces in the trash so Cal couldn't call or track him. Then he'd sat in the passenger seat as Ken drove them home and looked out the window, his mind replaying everything that had happened.

Ken hadn't said a word when Brady walked directly into the shower and started the water, leaving it so hot it burned as he took off his clothes and the drops hit his bare skin.

He was so…what? Disgusted? Angry? Ashamed of himself for not checking to see if any of those men hooked to the wall wanted to leave too? And Cal. He'd eaten with that man and he just… How could people live like that? It was all so ugly.

When he finally turned off the water, Ken was holding out a towel for him. Brady took it, raking him hungrily with his gaze.

Ken's hair was damp and loose—he must have showered in the office—and the pajama bottoms he wore were white, sheer and loose.

He looked like an angel.

Brady let go of his towel and reached for his lover, kissing him, worshipping him with his lips and tongue. He walked him back toward the bed and sat him down, dropping to his knees on the floor in front of him.

Ken put his hands in Brady's hair. "I'm so sorry. I never should have asked—"

Brady looked up abruptly and his expression made Ken go silent. "I need you."

The man was everything beautiful and right in the world.

He was everything.

"I need you," Brady repeated, reaching for the tie at

Ken's waistline.

Ken nodded, his wet hair draping damply over his shoulders as he lifted his hips and let Brady slip his pants off. He didn't resist when Brady spread his legs and moved closer, lowering his mouth onto Ken's stirring erection.

Yes, he sighed as he took Ken's cock in, groaning around the flesh as it hardened and filled his mouth. He closed his eyes and savored the taste of him. Clean and spicy. Hot and addicting. His hands moved beneath Ken's thighs and he kneaded the flesh, loving the hard muscle beneath the smooth, silky skin.

Need you.

Struggling for breath and fighting against his own arousal, Brady pulled back long enough to lift Ken's legs until his back was on the mattress, then spread them wide. He lay down between them and pressed his own erection into the bed, hungry for Ken. All of him. He opened his mouth over the tight sac at the base of Ken's shaft. The taste made him linger, and he rolled and teased the heavy balls with his tongue as he stroked Ken's erection slowly.

"Brady," Ken moaned softly, threading his hands through Brady's hair again and again.

He trailed his tongue up Ken's cock, tracing every ridge and vein, taking his time as he gazed directly, shamelessly, into dark golden eyes. *Need you*, he thought, licking the pre-cum that had leaked from the tip.

He rocked his hips into the mattress as he wet his finger in his mouth, then sucked Ken again while he lowered his hand between those strong legs and pushed inside the tight hole he loved.

Ken moaned, louder this time, and his legs went over Brady's shoulders, heels digging into his back. "*Yes.*"

Brady added another finger, thrusting them both through the tightly flexing muscles in a rhythm that matched the strokes of his tongue on Ken's cock.

Need you, Ken. Need this.

Love you.

Ken's body was arching off the bed, writhing as Brady sucked harder and pumped his fingers deeper. Faster.

"Brady, I'm close, baby," Ken gasped. "Do you want me to come in your mouth?"

Brady moaned, nodding. *Fuck, yes. Please, yes. Come in my mouth. I need to have this, taste this. I need to know this is mine.*

Ken's fingers dug into his scalp and his hips started pumping off the bed. Tears slipped from Brady's eyes as the head of Ken's cock swelled and hit the back of his throat. Oh and again. *Yes. Come.*

"Oh God, Brady. *Yes.* Fuck, I love it. I love…"

The hot burst of cream filled Brady's mouth and he drank it down hungrily, his hips still pumping against the mattress helplessly. Ken's taste was as addictive as everything else about him. It tasted like shameless lovemaking and heated passion. It tasted like heaven, so far from where he'd been.

He wanted to stay like this. Stay with Ken.

When Brady finally lifted his head, Ken was watching him with dilated eyes and skin tinged a darker honey with desire.

"Thank you," Brady said quietly. He got up and stared at Ken's lean, beautiful body, taking it all in before turning to rifle through his duffel bag for something to wear.

"No, thank *you.* That was amazing." Ken sat up and reached out to caress his hip, making him shiver. "I think the least I can do is return the favor. Let me help you with that."

Brady shook his head, despite the ache of his

erection. "Tempting, but not yet. I'm good. That was what I needed."

Ken stood and took his clothes out of his hands, dropping them on the floor. He slid his fingers through Brady's and squeezed. "You need more than that. I think we could both use some comfort food with this mission report. And then? Then I'll need more of you."

They ended up on the couch wrapped in blankets and each other, sharing a pint of mint chocolate chip ice cream.

"Are you ready to tell me about it?" Ken asked calmly.

"I cloned the phone. Varg—"

"No. I want to know everything, from the beginning. Whatever comes to mind. No rush, Finn. We're just talking."

He didn't want to talk about any of it, not after something that beautiful, but he knew it was necessary. He tried to shut down his emotional reactions and describe every scene, every person and every word spoken in graphic detail. *Just a mission report*, he told himself. *You've done this a million times.*

But when he finished telling Ken about the people on

the racks, he had to stop and ask, "Is that normal? Does that happen at your club?"

Ken had swirled his spoon through the ice cream and sighed. "Kink is, by definition, abnormal. In fact, that's a point of pride in most BDSM communities. Normal is the thing to avoid."

"You know what I mean. Have you ever experienced anything like that?"

Ken's nod was resigned. "I got into it in college, following a man I fell in love with, so at that time bondage and pain play was a purely sexual experience for me. Something I explored with him. He was a hard player, so I dove into the deep end without looking."

Brady lost his appetite and set his spoon down, but he didn't say a word. He'd asked for this. He wanted to know.

"When I moved back home, I kept going because of the community. I live most of my life in front of my computer screens, so that connection?" He held up his hand as if reaching for it now. "That connection has always meant everything to me."

Ken leaned back, his gaze drifting over Brady's face. "As far as my focus, I had been fascinated with rope work from the start. For me it's the most intimate type of bondage. It isn't loud or flashy—it's intense and beautiful, and in its purest form, the ultimate expression of trust. I traveled to other countries and learned from every expert I could find." Ken's laugh was laced with self-mockery. "I don't like doing something if I can't be the best. I'm a perfectionist."

As if Brady didn't already know that.

"What you saw, Finn? I wish I could tell you something different, but that's not exclusive to that club or our personal group of villains. Some people actually do crave that level of pain and humiliation. I've witnessed scenes more extreme than what you've described, and I know for a fact that in that case, it was something they wanted, something they requested during negotiations."

When Brady scowled, Ken shook his head. "I could go into their reasoning, try to explain it but there's no point because that isn't *my* scene. Even when I was younger and let people play me, I wanted what you... Well, I didn't enjoy clothespins or mousetraps, we can leave it at that."

"Does anyone play you now?"

Ken reached out to touch him, a soothing caress. "No. I'm a trainer and mentor now. I do demonstrations, like the one you saw at Burke's. People can experience sexual arousal and satisfaction in my ropes, and I love helping them if that's what they need, but I don't respond in kind. Maybe I've been doing it for too long. I need more."

The way he was looking at Brady made it clear what he was referring to. That and the pictures he'd painted about trust and intimacy in the ropes made Brady shift uncomfortably, still aroused from their earlier embrace. "I didn't mean to go off topic. There's a lot I need to tell you."

After Brady went through his time as a prize bull—during which Ken winced and leaned over to kiss him—he told him about Cal's initiation into the club. When it started, how they treated him, even his reaction to Brady's concern. Something in Ken's expression made him stop.

"What is it?"

"The timing. The assistant to the senator who brought down Burke getting an invite to the dark side at the same time I'd just started compiling Burke's locked files and sending encrypted copies to my contacts in the agency."

Brady frowned. "You think this is about Stephen? They talked about him."

"It isn't Stephen. Burke was Stephen's white whale. He wasn't looking into the others."

"But Cal isn't connected to you at all."

"I helped you with Burke's blackmail attempt on the senator." Ken paused. "Cal and I have a shared interest in another Finn as well. You."

Brady shook his head. "If they knew about you, they wouldn't have hired you as a rope guy, right?" He shuddered. "Though after seeing their version of rope I'm glad that was canceled."

Ken set down the ice cream and stood, starting to pace. "That's the other thing. Cal's jealousy aside, he knew who I was. That we were living together. If he did, they must have. Why let me think I'm going to be allowed in, with a whole group of big players in town? It doesn't make sense."

"Maybe we're reading too much into this." The sinking feeling in Brady's gut when he remembered those confident smiles told him they weren't. "Maybe it was just a coincidence."

Ken walked out the door of his loft and Brady followed as he went into his office and sat at one of the monitors, his fingers flying over his keyboard. "I should be able to weed through this Vargas info in a day.

Maybe we can find something—"

Beep.

Ken's fingers froze on the keys. "Vargas just got a new text message."

Brady put his hands on Ken's shoulders, needing to touch him. "It's probably from Cal. Those two were arguing over a guy a few hours ago and my phone is in bits in the trash."

The message popped up in a window on Ken's monitor directly from the synced-up clone phone. Brady read it silently, his fingers digging into Ken's flesh. Then he read it again.

Terry Wahl

346 Alpine Way

Entrance code:019

"Damn it!" Ken slammed his hands on the keyboard and pushed back his chair, causing Brady to move out of the way. He stood, whirling around to stare at all his monitors with two expressions Brady had never seen on his face.

Fear and doubt.

Brady tried to reach for him. "Relax, Tanaka. Come on, man, talk to me."

"They knew. They knew who I was looking for, what

I had, what we were planning. They looked into your eyes knowing this was what was going to happen. They *played* us."

That was Brady's first instinct. It made sense. "I just don't know how."

Ken gestured toward the room around them. "They found a way in. Or one of my agency contacts works for them. All of this needs to be destroyed. Tonight. I'll have to rebuild everything."

"What about Terry? The address? It could be real." Brady took Ken's hands, holding him. Steadying him.

"It could be a trap," Ken said, "but then any idiot with a brain cell would know I'd think that. If I called in federal help, that could blow up in my face too. At least until I know who my mole is."

"Solomon."

Ken looked at him as if he were insane.

"Chief of Police Solomon Finn the Younger. I don't think they'd expect a street full of squad cars. He could have that place surrounded in fifteen minutes."

"Terry could be dead by now. Or in another country. There's no guarantee he's there."

"There's another option. I've met these men. Maybe they decided to cut their losses. That they don't care enough about keeping him to risk you using your connections and calling in all those favors the government owes you." Brady dragged Ken along as he walked back to the loft and their clothes. "We have to take the chance. They know now. We'll never get an opening like this again. Not soon enough."

"You're right. Damn it, you're right. I'll get dressed. Use one of my burner phones to call your brother. I want to be there in case…"

"We'll be there." Brady prayed to God that Terry was too.

***

Solomon stood in Ken's living room, watching the news and looking stiff and uncomfortable. The uniform looked good on him. His straight, broad shoulders and slender frame gave him an air of authority despite his age—thirty-seven was young to be the Chief of Police, at least according to the forty-year-olds still working the beat. But Younger was a born leader. If only he smiled and went out on dates once in a while.

Still, he was a hero this morning. Last night he'd come in like the Calvary to save the day. Luckily there hadn't been a standoff—only one confused and frightened man waiting for them behind the door of the empty house. Terry Wahl.

Brady walked over to his brother and handed him a cup of coffee.

"Thanks," he said absently, looking around the room. "Where are the walls?"

Brady quirked his lips. "He doesn't own any."

His brother rolled his dark blue eyes and took a sip of the steaming brew. "How are they this morning?"

He was referring to Terry and his mother Patricia, Brady knew. Ken was with them right now. They were downstairs, having one last conversation before Trick took them away.

"As well as you might imagine."

There'd been no sleep last night after Terry had given his statement and Ken had insisted they all come back to the warehouse. Patricia couldn't let go of her son and Terry was practically catatonic.

It was heartbreaking. Ken's foster brother had fresh scars everywhere Brady could see skin, and his face was gaunt and haunted. He wouldn't wish that on anyone—coming back from the horrors of war only to fall into a personal nightmare. It was a miracle he'd survived both, though Brady suspected he wasn't feeling that lucky at the moment.

Ken had been a rock. He'd sat beside them and talked in a soft comforting voice as he told them about his plans to keep them safe. Brady had tried to stay out of the way, but Patricia had joined him in the kitchen to thank him for his help in the rescue.

"Kenneth told me you were in Afghanistan," she'd said. "That you had nightmares."

"Have," Brady corrected gently. "But he's making sure your son has the best care money can buy when you get where you're going. You heard him. And Ken's told me how strong you are. With you on Terry's side, and some time, he'll get better."

Patricia's smile was weary but genuine. "He's alive and with me. We'll make that enough for now." She paused. "Kenneth talked about me? Then you and he— you two must be very close."

Brady hoped so. "He cares about you, I know that. He didn't want to let you down."

They'd both turned at the sound of Terry's sob and watched as he wrapped his arms around Ken and wept into his neck. Swaying slightly, Patricia had reached out to take Brady's hand. "He didn't. Remind him of this moment if he ever forgets. He gave me back my son."

Brady looked up, shaking off the memory as Ken came in the front door and walked slowly toward them. The cross around his neck was gone. "They're on the road. Thank you, Chief, for the escort."

Solomon set down his coffee and shook his head. "I didn't authorize an escort for people carrying forged documents and fake IDs. My men just happen to be going in the same direction."

Ken sent him a grateful smile. "Lucky for us."

Brady walked over and took Ken's hand. "You okay?"

"I'm fine." He slipped his hand out of Brady's and crossed his arms. "I'm sorry Terry wasn't able to give a detailed statement."

Solomon rubbed the back of his neck with a sigh. "I am too. From what little you two have told me, I would love to get my hands on those sons of a bitches. But I'm afraid something happened this morning that—"

The phone on his belt rang and Solomon answered it immediately. "Finn."

As he listened to whoever was on the other end, his frown deepened. "They couldn't have waited?" He turned around and reached for the remote, his eyes on the television. "Thanks for the heads-up, Stephen. I'll call you back."

"What is it?" And why did Brady have the sinking feeling that he didn't want to know?

Solomon just gave him a grim look. "How the hell do you turn up the volume with this thing?" he demanded, holding up the remote.

Ken took it from him and pushed a button so they could hear the voiceover accompanying footage of a hotel entrance roped off with yellow crime scene tape.

"Three men were found dead this morning in a downtown hotel room in an alleged double murder-suicide," the woman reported. "One of victims has been identified as thirty-year-old Calvin Grimes, a political consultant who worked most recently for local Senator Stephen Finn. The names of the other two victims, both males, have been withheld pending notification of next of kin. Police aren't releasing any details about the crime scene, but sources close to the investigation tell us Grimes appears to have shot the other two victims before turning the gun on himself. Senator Finn's office has released a formal statement from both the senator and his wife, expressing shock and offering condolences and prayers to the families of all the victims."

"Jesus." Brady's legs gave out beneath him and he

sank into the couch. "This can't be happening."

"Oh, it's happening," Solomon said grimly. "I was waiting until you'd gotten the Wahls safely on their way to tell you. No need to add to *their* anxiety."

Brady looked over at Ken, thinking he looked like a statue. Like he wasn't even breathing until he said, "When? And who are the other two?"

"The call came in before dawn," Solomon told him. "They've been identified as Anthony James and Edward Vargas."

"Holy shit, *Vargas*?" Brady ask, his voice rising in disbelief. "Heavyset guy with a beard?"

Solomon nodded. "And their names are basically the only personal information we have on them. Someone's done a very thorough job of whitewashing their histories. Deleting, actually. After the things Stephen said at dinner the other night, I was expecting Brady's name to come up when we started digging into Grimes, but there was nothing—no texts, no emails, no phone calls. Hell, Stephen told me the picture of Brady on Grimes' desk has been replaced with that James boy's."

Brady was in shock. The Slaver's Club had gotten rid of that much information in one night? He didn't know anyone other than Ken that could do that. That was a lot of damn trouble to go through to create their narrative. To make Calvin Grimes look like a murderer.

Obviously he'd been right about Cal being a fall guy, but he hadn't realized how far they were willing to go. Vargas and Grimes were dead. He'd bet the third guy was that poor soul Vargas and Cal had in the back room. Who was going to send sympathy to Anthony James' parents?

"They're cleaning themselves out of the room," Ken said in a quiet, emotionless monotone. "Sweeping their way out the door so no one knows they were here."

He sounded so tired that Brady wanted to carry him back to bed until this news blew over.

Solomon agreed. "The place where we found Wahl was owned by Vargas and there's nothing in there that ties it to anyone or anything else. With Grimes and Vargas dead, we've got nothing."

Ken rubbed his temples. "Brady was right. They gave me Terry so I'd back off. They gave Brady a pass so I'd know what they are capable of. What Cal texted and the pictures and videos he sent to Brady in the last few weeks was salacious enough to fill the newspapers for months. Brady would have been dragged into this story and hounded by reporters. *They* decided to give him a pass. And they wanted me to know how easy that was for them."

"That was my thought." Solomon nodded.

Ken's laugh was bitter. "They got rid of the two men I used to find Terry. To find them. I'd be willing to bet the club is shut down by now too. They are a well-oiled machine, aren't they?"

"They could have killed you," Solomon offered grimly. "You, Terry *and* my brother."

"They won't touch me," Ken shook his head absently. "Those connections I have? They wouldn't risk it."

"We'll find them," Brady promised, fueled by rage at this new injustice. "We know a few of their names, and I'll never forget their faces. Men that wealthy? With facial recognition we could track their every move. Plus, we know there are other clubs and—"

Solomon grabbed Brady's arm and shook it. "You move on them again over my dead body. Do you hear me? You are out of this as of now, Brady. Do you understand what's happened? Is it even registering in your brain? They killed three men without hesitation *just to prove they could*. From what you told me, they kidnap people and assault them, *just because they can*. They let you go. They took you out of the equation for whatever reason and that is where you're going to stay. Out."

Brady glared down at his older brother. "Is that an order, Chief? Isn't this what Sol trained us to do? Be good cops? Good soldiers? Help people? You didn't see the things I did. How they treated those men—"

Solomon swore, tightening his calloused fingers on Brady's arm. "I didn't hold my breath and say a prayer every time you took another tour in Afghanistan just so I could watch you die as soon as you got back. You don't want to be a cop anymore? Fine. And you did your time as a Marine. But this? This spy game you're playing with Tanaka? *It's too fucking dangerous.*"

"I agree."

At Ken's quiet words, Brady, who taken a breath to continue fighting his brother, let it out in a rush. "What?"

"This is over now." Ken stared at Solomon until he looked away and let Brady go. "I can't thank you enough for all you've done, Chief. If you wouldn't mind, Brady and I need to talk about this alone."

Solomon sent Brady an enigmatic glance then nodded, his long strides taking him to the front door of the loft, where he paused. "I'm sorry about this, Tanaka.

But what you did for them? Your foster family? That was… You did good."

Ken lowered his chin in a sharp nod. "I appreciate it. I know how important family is to the Finns."

"There'll be a car here for a few days. If you need anything else..." Solomon hesitated, looking uncomfortable for a moment before he turned and headed for the stairs, leaving the door open.

Brady had a knot in his stomach. "What just happened, Ken? I get Solomon being cautious, but we aren't really letting this go, are we? I mean, sure, take a beat and make a new plan, but we can't let them get away with what they've done."

No one had the right to choose who lived and died. To play God. The never-ending war had taught him that. All those lives, all those families destroyed—for what? So these men could have the freedom to sit in their towers and get rid of anyone that wasn't convenient? "We can't let them win."

"I won't." Ken wouldn't look at him. His fingers were curled into fists. "But there are a few things I need to take care of first."

He walked out the door Solomon had just disappeared through, heading, Brady knew instinctively, to the place that used to be his one true sanctuary.

Brady followed, but before he even made it to the hall, he heard the sound of shattering glass and metal. He paused in the office doorway, watching silently as Ken took what looked like a metal pipe to all his monitors. He kicked over his towers beat them with a force and ferocity that was disturbing, and smashed everything to pieces.

Finally, he couldn't watch anymore. "Ken, *stop*. Talk to me."

"I'm fine," Ken muttered through gritted teeth, kicking the wreckage on the floor around and picking up all his broken hard drives. "I didn't find anything. There was no way they could have bypassed my security."

"So it's one of your contacts? Then why are you doing this?"

"I'm just being thorough."

He went over to the small kitchenette and opened his microwave, trying to fit them all inside.

Brady came up behind him and wrapped his arms around Ken's biceps, tightening when he started to struggle. "Stop. Please, babe. Look at me. *Talk to me*."

"You don't have to stick around for the cleanup if it upsets you. The job is over. In fact, if it's okay with you

I'd rather be alone." His voice was so cold. So unaffected, despite his recent bout of destruction.

"You want me to go back to the loft? I can help with—"

"I want you to go."

Stunned, Brady loosened his arms enough to whirl Ken around so he could look in his eyes. He looked like he meant it. How was he doing that? "You're kicking me out?"

Ken's smile was a brittle version of the one Brady loved. "Don't look at it that way, Finn. We did the job. We reunited a mother and son. We kicked some ass and had some fantastic sex. That's time well spent, in my book."

"Fuck you, that was more than sex," Brady said, anger and doubt deepening his voice. "You know it was."

Ken sighed, pain racing across his expression before it hardened again. "What I know is that you and I never made any sense. You love your big, crazy family and I love my independence and kink—which you aren't really into. For the most part I'd rather be by myself with my thoughts or on my computer. You'd rather run errands and fix a roof for your cousin's boyfriend so you don't have to live alone."

Brady flinched and Ken shook his head. "I'm sorry, Brady. I don't mean it like that, but if you're honest, you've thought the same things. That's why you kept turning me down in the first place. If we hadn't been living together and working on such an intensely personal case, nothing would have changed."

"No." He didn't feel this way due to proximity or adrenaline, no matter what Ken said. "I'm not going anywhere. Not when you're like this. You're not—"

"*I'm fine*," he stressed. "But I admit this job took its toll. I need time to sort it out. To think about everything that's happened. I know you understand."

We're not the best fit.

I want you to go.

I'd rather be alone.

Brady didn't think there was another way Ken could say it without holding a large, neon sign. Yesterday he'd thought... But this morning Terry was safe, Grimes was dead and Tanaka wanted him to go.

"I don't believe—I mean I can't *understand* why you..." He took a deep breath, releasing Ken and stepping back. "But it's your place. Your call. If this is what you really want, Tanaka, then I guess there's nothing left to say."

"This is what I think I need." Ken turned to face the microwave again. "What we both need."

Brady stared at his lover's stiff back for what seemed like hours. He wanted to fight. He wanted to take Ken in his arms and remind him how good they were together. But in the end he just left the office and went to collect his duffel bag. The only thing that belonged to him. The only proof that he was ever here.

It was over. When the shock wore off he needed to be as far from here as possible. He didn't want Tanaka to see him shatter.

CHAPTER TEN

"Here's another root beer, Brady." Seamus set the bottle on the bar in front of him. "Are you sure you don't want something stronger?"

Brady shook his head. He needed to stay in control. Now more than ever. "This sugar high is better than a rum blackout. I *am* hearing a strange pounding in my ears though."

"Construction." Seamus sighed. "I can't wait to open up again. Owen's crew has done great work and it's only two days, but I'm ready for the dust to settle so I can reopen. I miss adult problems and drunks and appetizers that aren't shaped like stars and dinosaurs."

Brady couldn't help but chuckle. Super Dad needed a vacation. He glanced over at the new stage that had sprung up by the dartboards. "A place for a band, bigger bathrooms, a fixed roof... That's a lot for two days."

"They get paid well, and they each get one free drink a night for life. Apparently that was the right incentive."

Brady imagined it would be. "How's your dad doing with all this change?"

"Dad is proud, and before you ask everyone else is fine." His cousin leaned his elbows on the bar and frowned. "You, however, look like shit."

"Gee, thanks," Brady muttered. "At least I don't have little mustard fingerprints on the back of my shirt."

Seamus looked over his shoulder and swore. "How the hell did that happen? I put Penny and Wes in the shower *and* changed my shirt before I came here."

Solomon appeared beside Brady, tossing a set of keys on the bar and taking off his sunglasses before he sat down. "Sol says he didn't own a clean shirt outside of his uniform until Rory left home. Hey brother, what's new?"

Brady ground his teeth together. Solomon was the last person he wanted to see. "Other than me being wrong about the pub being closed for construction? I don't know, Chief. You tell me."

"I can't close to family." Seamus shrugged, setting an

iced tea down in front of Solomon, who nodded his thanks.

"Okay, let's think about what's happened since the last time you answered your phone. Uncle Shawn's a little down in the dumps. Owen and Jeremy are coming back the day after tomorrow, and Badass has been staying with him for the duration. You know how much he loves that dog."

Owen's dog was going to come back spoiled rotten with no Brady-the-babysitter to look after him when Owen wanted a nap. Shame. "I'll send a card."

"I also heard from Rory that you went to the VA to talk to someone about your sleeping problems."

Brady didn't respond, reminding himself to sock Rory in the jaw for gossiping. As for the doctor, he'd had to do something. Waking up from memories of car bombs and innocent casualties had never been easy, but they'd never been this hard. Now, every time he realized he was awake, he remembered that there wasn't a good reason to be. Ken wasn't beside him.

Talking to the doctor helped. He'd even made another appointment.

"If it means anything, I'm sorry."

"What?" Brady looked over at Solomon in mock-surprise. "Should I be taping this?"

Solomon frowned. "I'm not sorry I was worried about you. I *am* sorry if something I said made him... That wasn't my intention."

Brady looked back down at his bottle. He shouldn't be taking this out on his brother. Solomon isn't the one who sent him away. All he'd done was show up exactly when he needed him to. "You were there to help and that's what you did. I appreciate it, and I should've said it before now."

"I'll always help you, Brady." Solomon placed his hand on his brother's shoulder. "And I'll always be here if you need me, even when I'm worried, and even if I don't agree. You know that, right?"

"I do."

He never doubted his family. They didn't always understand him, and he knew Solomon didn't always approve of his decisions, but he stuck it out and never let him down. It was love, Aunt Ellen always said, more than genetics or Sol the Elder's obsession with the Finn name. Love kept them together as a family. Love was the glue.

But Brady was no longer sure Ellen was right. Unless she'd only meant a particular kind of love. Not the kind that was intense and full of passion—not the kind that was obviously one-sided. Ken had sent him away so easily. Shut him out and moved on with his life without looking back.

Brady had spent the better part of a week going over everything that had happened, what they'd shared, and he was no closer to understanding how something so powerfully profound and life changing for him could mean that little to Tanaka.

It had happened so fast—falling in love. He knew it could—Ellen and Shawn were proof of that. But when he looked at Owen and Jeremy, at Tasha and Stephen, he saw a whole life of shared memories and experiences mixed in with the romance. Maybe that was the real truth, the real key. Maybe all that was between them was chemistry. Passion. Maybe Ken was right and time would make it fade.

What did he know? He'd never been in love until now.

Brady forced the painful memories down and glanced up to find Seamus and Solomon watching him with matching expressions of concern. "I'm fine. Stop hovering."

"You know what Jake would say to that?"

"Jake is twelve."

Seamus ignored him. "Jake tells me fine never means fine unless you're talking about a girl. Or in your case, a man. He says whenever people say they're fine, it means that they are too worn out from crying to go over why life sucks so bad."

Solomon snorted. "He's a prophet, that one."

"*I* think so," Seamus replied with a glance at Brady. "He's also an eavesdropper, and overheard me mentioning Terry Wahl to Noah. When he found out Tanaka had a foster brother, he told me it made sense."

Brady frowned in confusion. "How's that?"

Seamus took out a rag to wipe the sawdust from days of construction off the bar. "You weren't around when my kids came into my life. Jake was the first. He was six going on sixty back then. Introverted and in pain, but smart. He was at my side when Penny and Wes were born a year later, and he was the first to hold Little Sean when I agreed to help Mira out of a tight spot. He's a special boy and he's always been a people watcher. He usually figures things out long before I do."

Brady would have described Seamus exactly the same way.

"You should get his advice before you date again,"

Solomon joked.

"Nice, Younger. I'm working here."

Brady sent him a look. "What did he say about Ken?"

"He said Tanaka was good at everything because he has to be. When you don't know what it's like to have family to rely on and people you trust, you're all you've got."

There was a lump in Brady's throat. "He's a smart kid."

"He likes Uncle Necky," Seamus said chuckling. "All the kids do. Lord knows I owe him a kidney for the way he helped with Little Sean."

"We all owe him for that," Solomon agreed. "And I owe him for giving me back my brother."

Brady lowered his brows and looked at Solomon, wondering if he'd gone crazy. "What are you talking about, Younger? I'm *back* now? Forgetting the fact that it's been eight months since I took off the uniform, I'm still homeless and unemployed. I still have bad dreams and I'm still not returning to the police force the way you and Sol want me to. Nothing's changed."

Solomon's smile was subtle, but for him it might as well have been a parade. "I never cared about that. Dad might still give you shit about it, but that wasn't what I was looking for." He paused for a moment, and when he spoke again his voice was thick with emotion. "You were gone a long time, Brady. Even when you got home... Don't tell me I wouldn't recognize my own brother when you finally came back."

Damn it. "Don't start, Solomon. I can't..." His laugh was watery and rough. "Great. I'm back to my old self again, just in time to get kicked in the teeth by everybody's favorite hacker. What am I supposed to do now? He's smart and sexy and I love him and none of that means shit because *he* sent me away."

"He's a fucking idiot for being such a genius," Seamus frowned. "But I expect more from you. You heard what I said right? He isn't used to family. Isn't used to having people to lean on."

"Yeah?"

"Let me remind you about the advice you gave to Owen a few weeks ago after taking a bath in rum. You're a Finn, you said. We go all in or not at all. *All in or not at all.* Do those sound like the words of a man who'd let a little thing like being sent away for your own good get in your way?"

"You think he sent me away for my own good?"

Seamus glanced at Solomon, who nodded. "A part of

you thinks it too, otherwise you would have taken my calls. Think about it, Brady. You were there, looking into those men's eyes, close enough to touch them. And Tanaka is the one that put you there. The same men who smiled at you were responsible for that blood-soaked crime scene we found only hours later, and erasing your connection to Grimes. It crossed my mind they could erase you just as easily, which is why I lost my temper."

Still… "He told me to leave so casually, like I'd just been there to install a fucking light bulb."

"My guess is he knows you," Seamus offered kindly. "You're a big man with a big heart, Brady. If he'd showed you how much it hurt him, nothing he said would have convinced you to leave."

That big heart started to race. Like it was waking up for the first time in days. He looked over at Solomon. "What about you? Do you think I should go all in? What if things aren't over with the Slaver's Club? What if we have to deal with those bastards again?"

Solomon shook his head. "I hope that day never comes, but I'm not an idiot. And I know you're not the kind of man that walks away from a fight. Not when it matters." He lifted one shoulder. "If it gets too dangerous… *If* that happens, don't forget you've got family who loves you. And some of us own guns."

Brady got up from the bar stool and slung his arm around Solomon's shoulders. He got a lot of flak for being too uptight, but Brady knew that he'd been the one to raise them. Not their father. Solomon had forgone fun and a life of his own because he had five brothers to take care of. "Thank you, Younger."

"I told you I hate that nickname. Now stop drowning in your root beer and act like a man. And just be happy, damn it."

A few hours later, he wondered if Chief Finn would approve of the fact that his first attempt at being happy included breaking and entering.

He hadn't really had a choice, Brady told himself as he jabbed with his left, the force of his blow jarring his shoulder. Ken wouldn't answer his phone and Brady had never thought to make a spare key to the warehouse.

Throwing out another punch, he wiped the sweat off his face with his forearm—since his hands were encased in Ken's MMA sparring gloves—and scowled. Where was Tanaka right now? It was still light out, but maybe the club was already open. Maybe he should call Tasha and see if she knew someone there who could find out.

Someone who could tell Brady if Ken was busy "playing" with someone. If he seemed relieved to have things back to normal.

And maybe you could act like a grown man with balls instead of a teenage girl. Tighten up, Marine. He'll have to come home eventually.

He hadn't been planning it. Breaking in. But Trick wasn't the only one who knew how to pick a lock, and when the police didn't show up in the first twenty minutes, Brady knew Ken hadn't reset his security systems since he smashed the hell out of his hard drives and disconnected the cameras. It was going to take some elbow grease to get this bat cave up and running again. Ken would need help with that.

"Jesus," he muttered, punching the heavy bag more aggressively and finishing off the combination by driving his knee hard into his imaginary opponent's ribcage. He was pathetic.

Brady danced around the bag, throwing kicks and elbows, trying his best to wrench it from the steel anchor it swung from. Trying and failing to work off his nerves. He'd been doing a lot of that since he got here. Push-ups. Pull-ups. Jump rope. Weights. He'd gotten so drenched he'd taken off his t-shirt, and then his jeans, until all he had on were his boxers.

"If he doesn't get home soon, I'll go for a naked run, get arrested and he'll never know I was here."

And now you're talking to yourself.

He couldn't help it. Couldn't shut down his mind. There was a part of him that worried he was making a fool of himself. That coming here on secondhand advice of a twelve-year-old and his perpetually single older brother was not the smartest move. Particularly since it hadn't been his decision to leave in the first place. *Ken* had said they might not be the best fit. *Ken* had said that they both needed time to think about everything that had happened.

Ken had asked him to leave.

But he hadn't asked Brady what *he* wanted. He drove his knee deep into the bag, then swung his other leg around in a powerful kick that rung the iron rafter above his head. He reached out his hand to stop the wild swaying of his canvas enemy.

Ken didn't know what Brady was feeling, because he'd never gotten the chance to tell him. There'd been too much going on.

He'd wanted to. In the middle of the ugly mess they'd fallen into—a mess that still wasn't cleaned up—

Brady had wanted to tell Ken he loved him.

Seamus was right. He was an all or nothing kind of guy. He couldn't just turn his feelings off because they might put him in high-risk situations at some point in the future. He wouldn't live like that. And Ken might call him a fool, but Brady wasn't going anywhere until that man knew exactly what he was sending away.

"*Finn?*"

Thank God. Brady brought down his gloved hands and looked over his shoulder. "Tanaka," he acknowledged. "Busy day?"

"What are you... Did you forget something?"

Not exactly a warm welcome, but Brady would work with it. "I didn't forget anything. What's in the box?"

"My new office." Ken set down the box of computer parts he was carrying and stalked toward Brady, those usually wicked lips tight and thin. "You don't have a key."

"No, I don't. We'll need to fix that when I move back in."

"I told you to go."

"And now I'm back."

When Ken's torso twisted and his leg swept out, Brady was ready for him. He side stepped the kick, wrapped his arms around Ken's shoulders and they fell together. Brady rolled until he was on top, his legs straddling Ken's hips and arms so he couldn't move. "This feels familiar," he laughed.

Ken bucked beneath him. "Damn it, Brady, this isn't funny. Why are you here?"

"Because you need me."

He stilled at that. "I don't. I'm backing off, for the moment anyway. I'm rebuilding and recoding and— They won't try anything now. I have time to find out who—"

"No." Brady shook his head, cutting off Ken's words. "Not for that."

"What else?" Ken's eyes were slightly dilated and his breathing was shallow. "I mean, I don't need any—"

Brady kissed him. Closed his eyes and felt everything inside him melt when Ken sucked his tongue deep into his mouth as if he couldn't help himself. As if he'd missed him just as much. *Yes.* Something that strong didn't go away overnight.

He lifted his head and Ken moaned, shaking his head. "That doesn't prove anything. I don't I need you. And you don't need the trouble I'd come with."

Brady looked into Ken's eyes and smiled. "You

thought you knew what we needed before. You thought sending me away was the right thing to do, but you were wrong. I know *exactly* what you need."

"Sex won't solve these problems."

"You need someone who isn't intimidated by that brain of yours, or that mouth," Brady was trying to ignore that mouth so he could finish. "You need to be dragged to chaotic family dinners and get the third degree from people who care a little too loudly. You need someone who'll take you by the side of the road, in the shower, anywhere he can have you because he can't get enough."

Ken opened his mouth as if to interrupt. Brady couldn't touch him like he wanted through his gloves, so he kissed him again. When they were both breathless, he lifted his head and whispered, "You don't need to be alone, genius. What you need is someone who loves you. Someone who didn't think he *could* love like this. Not this much. Not so completely. And that's me, Tanaka. I'm the right guy for the job. The only guy. I also still happen to be unemp—"

"Shut up." Golden eyes closed and Ken took a shivering breath. When he opened them again, Brady saw something in them that gave him reason to hope. "I need my arms back, Finn."

"Shit. Sorry." He rolled, getting to his feet and bringing the strap of one glove up to his teeth. He was already edgy, and aroused from being this close to Ken. He didn't need to add *stuck in boxing gloves* to that list.

Ken stood up with him. "Give those to me."

Brady held out his arms.

"How long have you been in here?"

"A few hours."

"Why didn't you wait in the loft?"

Brady's cheeks heated. "I thought this way I wouldn't *really* be invading your privacy."

"So you'd only be breaking in my gym, not my house?" When he nodded, Ken chuckled and reached for the other glove. "You really are a giant Boy Scout."

He shrugged. "Cops...Marines...we're all just bigger, older versions. We still get badges when we're good and everything."

The last glove came off and then Brady felt Ken's hand slip inside his boxer shorts, his fingers sliding over his erection. "Have you been good, Brady?"

Fuck. "I might lose my badge if you keep doing that."

Ken stopped touching him long enough to drag his

own shirt off over his head, and then he was pulling Brady's head down for another kiss. "Fuck the badge."

Brady groaned and wrapped his arms around Ken's hot body, turned to press him against the gym wall. That mouth. Damn, he'd missed that talented mouth. He tilted his head and let their tongues tangle, his hands brushing Ken's as they both fought to get his pants unbuttoned.

"I should shower."

"Don't you fucking dare."

"Upstairs," Brady gasped. "The lube's upstairs."

Kicking off his pants, Ken turned in Brady's arms to face the wall and then thrust back with his hips as he bent forward. "Now. Fuck me right now, Brady. I can't wait that long."

Brady shuddered. "Tanaka…"

"Finn, please. Don't make me take you down. *Fuck me*."

That was all he needed to hear. He gripped Ken's hips, spread his cheeks with his thumbs and dropped to his knees, sliding his tongue wetly over that tight hole he loved. So good. He wanted to make this good.

"Yes," Ken moaned. "Damn it, Finn you make me crazy. You don't know how many times I thought about th—*God*. Do you want me to beg again? I'll beg." Brady pushed his tongue inside Ken's ass.

"*Christ*, yes, okay, I'm begging you. I need that big, thick cock in my ass. Don't you remember how tight it was? How good? I need it. I need you to fuck me until I forget my name, forget you weren't here—*yes*. Brady, baby, please."

Climbing up to stand on shaky legs, Brady wet his palm with his tongue, sliding it over his erection. Ken's cries had destroyed the restraint he'd been clinging to, and now Tanaka was going to get what he'd asked for.

They both shouted when he thrust inside, muscles wound tight and shaking as he filled and stretched Ken's ass until he was all the way in.

"*Brady*."

"*Fuck*. No, Ken don't move."

But Ken wouldn't listen, pushing his hips back and swiveling them seductively. He looked over his shoulder and Brady saw the wild need, the mischief in his eyes. "If you don't want me to move, Finn, then hold me down."

Brady dragged them both to their knees and pushed Ken down until his face met the floor, then held him there with a hard grip on the back of his neck, under his braid. "Like that?"

"*Yes*."

He'd needed this so much. Needed Ken. He'd wanted this to be perfect, instead he was covered in sweat and pinning his lover to the ground like an animal ready to rut.

"Fuck," he swore, gripping Ken's shoulder tightly with his free hand as he gave in to the call of the damn wild.

"*Yeah*. Oh, Brady, you're so good. I can't get enough. *Faster*. Yes, like that. Don't stop fucking me. Don't stop. Never stop."

Never. He would never fucking stop. Brady flexed his ass and pumped his hips in a rhythm that was no longer controlled. He felt primal. Possessive. His fingers tightened and Ken quaked beneath his touch.

"Mine," Brady muttered low and dangerous.

"Yes," Ken moaned back. "Yes, you bastard, I'm yours."

Ken's easy submission stole the last of his control. "Say it again."

"Anything you want. I'll do *anything*. I'm yours, Brady. *Fuck*, I'm—"

Ken cried out and Brady knew he was coming. Knew he had to join him. "*Yes*."

Mine.

Brady wasn't sure how long he'd laid there on the floor, wrapped around his lover, his cock still buried inside him.

His. Ken was his.

He hasn't said it back.

"You've started thinking already," Ken murmured, clearly amused. "I'm impressed, Finn. I'm still not sure I have."

"I was thinking about negotiating a scene." Hopefully he'd worded that correctly.

Ken tensed against him. "Brady, I don't know if that's a good idea."

"I think it is."

Rolling away, Ken leaned on his elbows and looked down at him with wary golden eyes. "I don't have the right to ask after the things I said, but tell me the truth. Do you really think you're ready, or do you just want to please me?"

Brady hesitated. "That's a trick question. Of course I want to please you. And I want to share in the things you love because I…" He swallowed. "If you'd asked me a month ago, I would have said it was never going to happen, but now I can't stop thinking about it. I have been for a while. I want to know how it feels to have your hands on me, to have you in control. I want so much, with you, from you, but I'm always getting in my own way by thinking too much. The psychiatrist said something about me carrying too much weight. Not physically but—"

Ken pressed a finger against his mouth. "You went to see someone? About the nightmares?"

He nodded.

"And did you tell him you were thinking about being tied up?"

Brady blushed. "Surprisingly? He was not surprised. And he knew more about it than I did. Even printed out some articles on the subject."

Ken lowered his hand to Brady's chest, tangling his fingers in the hair there. "You're serious about this, aren't you?"

"I am."

"Okay then." Ken leaned down to kiss his chin. "Hold that thought."

Ken got to his feet and walked quickly toward the stairs. Brady watched his ass from beneath his lashes, unable to keep the smile off his lips. There wasn't a doubt in his mind that Ken never would have approached this on his own. He had no desire to push Brady into something he didn't want.

He was the better man.

Brady was anxious, but excited. He'd read about the cathartic release of rope for people with PTSD and the feeling of safety, but anytime he thought about Ken tying him up and touching him—well, his thoughts weren't all that therapeutic.

He heard Ken's footsteps echo on the gym floor and looked over to see him carrying a large cloth bag. "Brady? Why don't you take the heavy bag down and set it against the wall."

Brady frowned, his stomach knotting. "Why?"

Ken's lips curled in a little smile at he set his bag down. "We haven't negotiated yet so I'll answer. When you don't have all the amenities that are available at the club, you have to improvise. You're a big man, Brady. I'm improvising, but I think you'll enjoy it."

Brady jumped to his feet and wrapped one arm around the bag and used his free hand to open the catch of the metal D-ring that secured it to the rafter. He grunted as he lifted it and slipped the ring out of the eye-hook above. As he set it where Ken had indicated, he looked back up at the hook. It was thick, heavy-duty steel—strong enough to hold the weight of the bag, and strong enough to bear his weight as well. "Huh."

Ken laughed. "Changing your mind already?"

"No."

"Good. We need to set some ground rules. What *don't* you want to experience?"

"Whips," Brady answered quickly. "No whips." He would never be curious about that.

Ken nodded, pulling out several lengths of blue nylon rope.

Oh God.

"You're new at this, so let me tell you what I want. Nothing but you, me and the rope. We're going to start very simply. Just so you can feel the weight of it and understand that, though ultimately you're in control, you're giving that control over to me temporarily."

Shit. Focus. "Yes. Just us and rope. Got it."

"It might be an emotional experience for you. You hold back—everyone does, and sometimes things come out. I'm telling you now so you know it's okay with me. You can trust me with that."

He'd read about how deeply affecting rope could be. "I trust you completely."

Ken nodded, looking pleased. "You can't argue or question my commands, but you can stop me with a safe word."

"Apple pie," Brady said without thinking. Then he laughed. "Don't tell Tasha that's my safe word."

Ken's gold eyes were sparkling, his cheeks slightly flushed. "I promise. Now about sex."

"Sex?" Brady swallowed hard.

"I've told you I don't usually mix the two, but in your case I'm making an exception. While you're tied up, would you be okay with me touching and sucking your cock?"

"God, yes."

"What about your ass? Can I use my tongue? My fingers? Can I give it a tap or two with my hands?"

He swallowed. "Okay."

"That's good. Then we can begin. From now on, Brady, I'm in charge. You need to do what I say and answer my questions honestly. Can you do that?"

"Absolutely."

"Then step directly under the hook and hold out your arms, wrists together."

When Brady obeyed, Ken began to swiftly and expertly bind his wrists together. Brady tried to focus on the knots but his eyes were blurring a little.

"Breathe, Finn. Breathe for me. I'm here."

Realizing he'd been holding his breath, he inhaled deeply and tried to relax. His breath caught again when Ken dragged a chair over and climbed onto the seat so he could tug Brady's arms over his head. He slipped the rope through the round metal anchor on the rafter above and dropped it behind Brady. Ken looked into his eyes and smiled, stroking his cheek before he hopped down and strung the rope over to a large bolt sticking out of the concrete wall. Brady had to stretch his arms and felt like he was one tug away from his heels leaving the ground as Ken tied the nylon cord off.

It exposed him. Made him vulnerable. Open to whatever Ken wanted to do to him. He let out shaky breath as he felt adrenaline push his heartrate up a notch.

"That is sexy as hell, Finn," Ken murmured hotly as he stepped back in front of Brady and moved the chair out of the way. Caressing Brady's hip with one hand, he added, "Your body was made to be displayed. Used. Enjoyed."

Hardly. "More like made to carry heavy things and knock down doors."

"I don't think I said you could disagree with me."

Ken's fingers dug into his hip in warning. "You have this image of yourself that's all wrong. You're no clumsy ox, Finn. And you're not just a battering ram. You're a big strong man who knows how to protect the people he loves. Who knows how to move to make his lover scream his name."

Brady's erection was getting harder to ignore. Ken noticed and wrapped it tight in one fist.

"Oh God."

Ken chuckled. "I'd say that's a good sign you're still with me. Are you ready for more?"

More of what? Did it even matter when Tanaka was touching him? "Yes."

Ken went back to his bag and stood behind Brady. He resisted the urge to turn and look behind him, instead focusing on his breathing. He could feel the weight of the nylon sliding over his shoulders, his stomach, between his legs, as Ken wove the rope around his body. Whenever Brady tensed, Ken would gentle him with a hand on his back or hip until he relaxed. Then he would start again.

There wasn't much talking so all Brady could do was feel. The weight of the knot in the center of his chest and the matching one on his back. The slide of two lines of nylon slipping between the cheeks of his ass.

This was starting simply?

"There." Ken tugged something and the rope around his waist and between his legs tightened, separating his ass cheeks. Rubbing against his increasingly sensitive skin.

A strange feeling traveled through his body and something started to shift in his mind, like a light turning on in the dark. With every heartbeat he felt more alive, more aware. The pressure from the ropes, the coolness of the air on his skin, the heat radiating off Ken's body…his awareness of everything had heightened in a way he'd never experienced. It was revelatory.

"Now we can play."

Brady slammed back into the present and gasped when Ken pressed up behind him, rising on the balls of his feet to grip the rope that bound Brady's wrists with one hand. Ken's cock—wet with lube—slid over Brady's skin. He rocked against him, his other fingers slipping between the ropes and rubbing the tight ring of his ass.

"*Fuck.*"

"Someday." Ken whispered the promise against Brady's shoulder. "I'm greedy, remember? I never want to give up the feeling of your big cock breaking me open, but I'm man enough to admit I've thought about returning the favor. Tell me the truth if you want a badge, Boy Scout. Have you ever let anyone bend you over?"

"Once."

"Did you like it?"

"I would with you," Brady breathed, knowing it was true.

Ken's body stopped pressing against his as he took a step back. "Someday," he repeated. "But now I need to know how you feel. Can you wriggle your fingers? Blood flowing?"

All his blood was flowing to his cock. He took a deep breath and forced himself to focus. "It feels a little like a dream," he said honestly. "Like I'm not entirely in my body, and when I am, I don't know what sensations are real. But everything is more sensitive, if that makes sense."

"I know that feeling," Ken soothed, stroking his skin and circling around to face him. Brady's body shivered under his delicate touch. "You may not think so, but I think you and these ropes were made for each other."

"I know who I was made for." He hadn't meant to

say it, hadn't known he was going to, but it was right. It felt right.

Ken looked up and gave him that Lucifer-before-he-fell smile. "I think someone deserves a reward."

Brady cried out when Ken leaned over and sucked in the head of his cock. It was so much more intense. Every lick, every light scrape of his teeth, was heightened. He took Brady all the way in, swallowing when he hit the back of his throat and moaning, sending the vibration to the base of Brady's spine. "Fuck, Ken. Oh God."

He couldn't move his hips, couldn't move. He couldn't lower his hands to Ken's braid and guide him. All he could do was breathe and groan and take whatever Ken gave him. All he could do was feel.

Brady couldn't stop moaning, the deep sounds rumbling endlessly in his chest, forcing their way out as Ken's lips brushed the base of his shaft. Taking it all. *Fuck, baby you're taking it all.* When Ken's hands slipped around to squeeze and massage the cheeks of his ass, Brady knew he wasn't going to last.

"Ken…Ken, I'm close."

Tanaka moaned again and sucked hard, and Brady started to shake. "Please. Please, baby. Deeper. Oh yeah, I'm so close…I can't—*Ah, yes*. I love it. Love it so much. Love you so much. *Fuck!*"

Live wires and lightning and fucking rockets shooting into the sky. It was too much. Everything he was feeling, like he would shatter, like he had never been more whole…all of it happening at once and sending him hurtling into space.

His first thought, when he could form one, was that if this was what rope was like, he might definitely be kinky.

A few hours later, after a shower and dinner in bed, Brady rose up onto his elbow and looked down at Ken. "I was thinking…"

"Again?" Ken laughed, his body curled around Brady's in a loose embrace.

"I was wondering if you'd given any more thought to letting me have that job."

He didn't say *Do you love me?* He didn't want to push.

No, that was a lie. He didn't want to push Ken away. It might take time for someone as independent as Tanaka to embrace the idea.

Ken lifted his hand and slid his fingers through Brady's hair. "You want to know all my secrets, Finn?"

Brady tried to smile. "Just the one would do for now."

"That night when I brought you home, the night you can't remember? You were a perfect gentleman. You just talked. About your family, about not knowing where you fit anymore. You told me that you were waiting for the right thing. To do something that mattered. To have someone love you the way you were now."

Brady felt his throat close. "I'm really glad I don't drink anymore."

Ken shook his head. "No, it was beautiful. Everything you said was beautiful. And I knew that night that I might be falling for you. I wanted you since I saw you standing in the doorway guarding Tasha, but in that moment I wondered what it would be like to be loved by someone like you." He pulled Brady's head down to kiss him passionately, making his cock stir and his mind go blank before easing him away again.

"I don't have to wonder anymore. And neither do you. I love you and I need you. I belong to you. Whatever happens next, I want it to happen with you."

Brady groaned as Ken pulled him down for another kiss. "Good answer."

CHAPTER ELEVEN

Brady raised his voice so Seamus could hear him over the sounds of happy patrons and music. "Why are we having another Finn Again? And why is it in the bar?"

Seamus grinned proudly at the wall to wall crowd. "We're celebrating."

Ken joined them, his hand slipping instantly into Brady's. Where it belonged.

Seamus smiled at them both, then puffed out his chest until Brady and Ken noticed his shirt.

"Are you kidding?" Brady laughed. "Did Owen make that on his vacation?"

Seamus was wearing a Finn Club t-shirt. And of course there was a shamrock on it. Because anything connected to Owen had to be shaped like a shamrock or taste like pizza. "Where is he and how did he convince you to wear that?"

"He's on his way. But he didn't need to convince me. I got one of these for everyone. Even Uncle Necky." Seamus reached behind him and came back with two identical shirts, handing one to Ken before waving at someone else.

"Your family is crazy, Brady," Ken said as they walked back to their small table in the corner.

Brady smiled. "I know. But I promise, you'll learn to love it."

Ken winked at him and took off his shirt, baring his tattooed back to the packed room. Brady heard a few catcalls from male and female strangers who happened to be looking his way before Ken slipped the ridiculous t-shirt over his head, pulled out his braid and posed for Brady. "How does it look?"

Brady was blushing. "*Who's* the crazy one?"

"I am." Ken smiled his siren smile and slipped his fingers into the belt loops of Brady's jeans. "For you. Want to go check out the new restrooms?"

"Don't tempt me like that. Every member of my family is in this bar."

"Owen's not here yet."

And old Sol had told James he wasn't coming. Brady was disappointed, but not surprised. He'd wanted to introduce Ken to his father, but he knew it would happen eventually. Ken wasn't going anywhere. The rest of this Finn Club wouldn't allow it.

"Most of my family," he amended, looking around the room.

Ellen and Shawn both looked good after their recent health troubles. They were waltzing near the new stage where the band was playing. Stephen sat close to Seamus with Tasha cradled in his lap, caressing her rounded stomach as if he were holding the most valuable treasure in the world.

Rory was at the bar with an ER doctor who was separated from his wife, Wyatt and Noah were making Jen laugh...and Trick was leaning against the wall, not far enough away from her for Brady's peace of mind.

He couldn't find Solomon or James but he knew they were around here somewhere. His family. T-shirts. Seamus beaming like he had a secret... "Ken? Did anyone tell you what we're celebrating?"

Ken shook his head just as the band stopped playing and the sound of silverware tapping glass started to spread. Old Shawn kissed his wife and joined Seamus in front of the bar. "Welcome to Finn's!"

The crowd cheered.

"I'm old and retired, so I don't get a chance to join you that often. My son, the new owner, was kind enough to let me steal some of the spotlight." Seamus patted him on the back and Ellen blew him a kiss. The familiar sight made Brady smile.

"Ancient as I am," Shawn continued, "I've learned a little about life. The most wonderful thing about it is that every day we get a chance to make new memories, discover new reasons to come together, find new people to love, and maybe even fix a few mistakes along the way."

He paused and looked over at Solomon, who shook his head. Shawn's shoulders drooped for an instant—not long enough for most people to catch, but Brady noticed. Had he expected Sol to come?

Someday Brady was going to find out what had happened between them to cause this decades-long rift. But it obviously wasn't going to happen tonight. The Elder Sol was one stubborn son of a mule.

"Anyway, it's a beautiful night and I hear we have a lot to celebrate. So drink, eat and make sure you tip the band."

Everyone gave Shawn another round of applause, and then Seamus lifted a mug of beer. "Thank you to my father, the man who started this grand old pub, Shawn Finn. May I someday be that wise and that lucky to have such a beautiful woman on my arm."

Shawn crossed his fingers and Seamus laughed. "It's been one hell of a year," he told the crowd. "I've never been prouder of my family, or more inspired by the wonderful people they've found to share their lives. People who, for some unknown reason, love them enough to put up with all of us."

He pointed his glass toward Ken, and Brady laughed until Ken leaned over the table to kiss him.

"If all of you can hang in there just a little while longer, we have something really special in the works. But first, let's raise a glass to the Senator's wife, Mrs. Natasha Rivera Finn. I think she has something to say."

"Something is definitely going on," Brady said in Ken's ear.

"Clearly," Ken agreed with a smile. "It's called fun. Pay attention."

"Smartass."

Tasha was making the audience laugh with some racy

humor about her pregnancy, but once Brady started, he couldn't stop looking at Ken.

How had he gotten so lucky? Nothing in his life had prepared him for this kind of happiness. He still wasn't sure he deserved it. But that didn't mean he'd let it go without one hell of a fight.

Just like Ken, he was ready for whatever came next. And yes, he had a feeling they weren't done with that shadowy group of untouchables with blood on their hands. But Terry and Patricia were together and safe. Ken was safe and they were in love. For now, in this moment, life was good. Brady felt blessed. Happy. With this man by his side, he could do anything.

Ken must have felt him staring. "You're missing Tasha's comedy stylings," he said. "What is it?"

"Have you ever been to Paris? I told you about the place Mom had there. I was thinking we should take a vacation. We've earned it."

Ken leaned over and kissed him again with those perfect, wicked lips, making his heart skip. "I'd do Paris with you. Or you in Paris. Anytime, Finn. Anything you want."

"I love you."

"And I love you. I wasn't expecting this." He made a

motion to include the bar filled with Finns. "I thought I had it all together. Thought I was doing great on my own."

It was hard to argue with that. "You were Batman."

"Exactly." Ken's grin softened. "I was fine until I met you."

Brady smirked. "Jake says whenever people say they're fine, it means that they're too worn out from crying to go over why life sucks so bad."

"Jake? The tween? Well, it must be true then."

Brady nodded. "For the record, I was fine too. *Just* fine. All black shirts, control and careful passion. I didn't think there was anything more for me. Until you."

"Stop or I'll drag you out of here before we find out what's going on. You are trouble, Finn. A giant, gorgeous mountain of trouble. I should have known from the minute I saw you but I—*Oh,* wait, I think she's getting to the good part." Ken kissed him quick with a laugh, then turned his head back toward the bar.

"Time to get serious." Tasha brought her hand up to quiet the crowd. "I've known these delectable Finns for years now, and they have many wonderful qualities. Too many to be fair to the rest of us. Those eyes. Those bodies." She pointed at Ellen and Shawn. "Those parents." Everyone laughed. "But they aren't perfect. One of their *less* than wonderful traits is their need to be in your life. Not just involved. *In. Your. Life.* Little Finn knows what I'm talking about."

Jen raised her glass and smiled, nodding. Brady noticed Trick laughing with another man behind her. A cop he recognized. James' friend?

"So because everyone was *so upset* not to be present for what *I* thought was a very personal moment, we're going to put on a show for them right now, aren't we honey? Stephen? Baby, will you help me out?"

"He looks nervous," Ken murmured.

"She's Tasha and she's got the entire room's attention. *I'm* nervous."

Seamus set out a chair and Tasha guided Stephen into it. "Senator? Do you remember that time you found out I was pregnant?"

He grinned. "I do."

"Do you remember tearing up and kissing my stomach and singing Irish lullabies to it for over an hour?"

Stephen adjusted his collar, shaking his head at the crowd. "She's exaggerating." He sent her a warning look. "She's also a brat."

Brady watched Tasha share a look with Stephen's twin Seamus, who held a camera phone up to his brother's face.

"Uh-oh," Brady muttered. "I need to talk to him about that. All recording devices should be banned in this place."

Ken patted his thigh. "After tonight."

Tasha took Stephen's hand and placed it on her stomach. "I didn't get the chance to tell you with everything that's been happening, but the doctor asked me to come in for another ultrasound this week."

Senator Finn paled visibly, sitting up straighter in his chair. "Tasha?"

Her smile was incandescent. "It's okay, honey. I'm healthy. Everything's perfect." She paused. "We're just having twins."

The roar in the pub was deafening, but Brady didn't need to hear to read the expression of joy on Stephen's face. His blue eyes filled with tears as he stood, pulling his wife into his arms and kissing her senseless in front of God and everyone.

"We did that." Ken sounded proud of himself.

"We did *not* do *that*," Brady corrected him. "But we helped. I wonder if that gives us first dibs on baby names."

"Maybe we could make that the fifth rule of Finn Club."

"We'll see."

Ken's golden eyes were filled with laughter. He looked like he belonged here, in Brady's crowded and messy life. And Brady finally understood what Solomon meant when he said his brother was back.

Brady was home.

Turn the page for the Bonus Quickie,
A Curious Proposal.

A Curious Proposal
An Owen and Jeremy Quickie

OWEN

"Why won't you let me?" Jeremy moaned, his gorgeous tattooed ass in the air, taking every inch of Owen's aching cock.

"You don't like it, baby?" Owen gripped the handcuff chain and tugged teasingly, reminding Jeremy just who was in control, even here in the woods in the middle of nowhere. "Not knowing where I've brought you? If anyone is watching? If they know how easy it was to get you on your knees in the dirt with your pants around your ankles?"

"*Owen.*"

"The blindfold stays on...unless you want me to stop."

Jeremy pressed his forehead into the carry-on bag Owen had put there and relaxed in submission. "Don't stop," he whispered.

"What's that?" Owen closed his eyes, torturing himself as he slowed down, pulling back until only the head of his cock was inside Jeremy's snug ass. "I can't hear you."

"Don't stop," he said, louder, with an edge of anxiety and need.

"Don't stop what?"

"You are a goddamn sadist," Jeremy muttered.

Owen laughed, need making him light-headed. "It's taken this long for you to figure that out? Don't stop what?"

"*Don't stop fucking me, Master Finn.*" Jeremy's voice was so loud it startled a few birds in a nearby tree and made Owen smile. He only used "Master" when he was really desperate.

"You know I won't. I can't resist this tight, fuckable ass."

Owen looked down, spreading Jeremy's cheeks wide with his thumbs so he could watch his own lubed-up cock stretching that sexy ring of muscles gripping him like a hungry fist.

"Damn, I've needed this *all day*." He went in slow, one inch at a time, wanting to hold back as long as he could. Wanting this to last. "I've been planning it for hours, taking you like this."

"Hours?" Jeremy panted. "Deeper, Owen. *Please*."

"Be patient." Owen slapped Jeremy's hip with the palm of his hand. "I decided to cuff you when you rejected my mile high club suggestion."

But he'd been planning to wait until they got into the cabin he'd rented for their two-week vacation to put his plan in motion. His timetable had changed the minute he got that blindfold on Jeremy in the car. He'd been so turned on during the thirty-minute drive he'd barely been able to wait to put the damn rental in park.

Jeremy did this to him. Sex with him was always hot, hard and ecstatic, and it had been from the first time he got that big, beautiful cock in his hands. Owen could never get enough of his mouth or how good it felt to be taken by him. He craved making his lover crazy enough to go primal. Craved submitting to Jeremy's wild, rough claiming. Sometimes he needed it so badly he wondered how he'd live without it.

Still, Owen liked getting the chance to turn the tables and take the lead. When he had control, he made sure he took his time. He'd tie or chain his lover up, paddle him or whip him with the small leather flogger Jeremy had gotten him as a present, and work on him until he was begging to be fucked. It was a challenge to resist the race to the goal line, but Owen loved a challenge.

He loved Jeremy.

He stopped, his erection still only partially in, and waited. His whole body was vibrating with restraint when Jeremy finally tried to push back. *There.* Owen spanked him again.

"I told you to be patient," he warned. "*I* was patient. I sat next to you for four hours in that deathtrap, rock-hard and needing you, and you were too busy reading to join me in the bathroom and suck my cock."

"They would have noticed," Jeremy panted. "We wouldn't have fit."

Owen slid his hand around Jeremy's hip and gripped that thick, delicious erection. "It's not easy, lover, not with that monster cock of yours, but you always fit."

"Owen, damn it."

"Not even a hand job under the blanket, Jeremy," he continued wickedly. "No one was looking. It would have been so fucking easy for you to slip your hand into my pants and give me some release. You know what your touch does to me. And you know I could have returned the favor." His fingers tightened around Jeremy's cock for a heartbeat, and then he let it go.

Jeremy swore again under his breath. "Stewardess," he gasped. "She would have done it."

"She *did* keep asking if I wanted anything else," Owen mused, pulling his dick back just enough to make his lover shake. "I wonder what she would have done if I told her. Or better, just fucking showed her. Unzipped you right there and given her a peek at what I was hungry for."

Jeremy bit his lip, his hands flexing in the cuffs. "You liked it. All that attention."

"I didn't want her," Owen growled. "I wanted this."

So much for winning this challenge, he thought as he drove his hips forward, filling Jeremy and starting a fast, deep rhythm that would end their session too damn soon.

"This was all that was on my mind," he muttered. "Burying myself in this tight ass over and over again. Getting you alone, finally alone and on your knees for me."

Trembling now, Jeremy rattled his cuffs. "Please."

Owen couldn't refuse him, undoing the handcuffs and letting them fall to the ground.

"Don't take off your blindfold," he ordered.

Jeremy was obviously too aroused to disobey as one

free hand went instantly to his erection. "Harder, Owen. I deserve it. I should have bent you over the drink cart and given you what you wanted. I need to learn my lesson."

Owen wanted to laugh at his tactics but he was too turned on. He slid his hand up Jeremy's spine, loving the slapping sound of flesh as he gave him what they both needed.

"That?" His knees sank into the dirt as he punished Jeremy with his cock. "You want to learn *that* lesson, baby? Is that the kind of fucking you deserve?"

"*Yes.*" Jeremy's arm was working as he stroked his own erection in time to Owen's thrusts. "Oh God, Owen, don't stop."

"You don't want to know where we are?"

"I don't care. I need it as much as you do. I wanted to bend over the seat and suck your cock so all the women eyeing you knew I could. Can I come, Owen? I need to come."

"Almost," Owen allowed, his voice guttural. "I'm almost there. I just need... Fuck, that's good. I just need a few more— *Now.*"

He heard Jeremy's voice break on his name, and his head fell back with the power of his climax, his hips pumping in time with the waves of his release. *Yes. Love this. Love you.*

When he could hear himself think over the rush in his ears, he gently pulled out, smiling with satisfaction as he dragged his t-shirt off over his head and used it as a towel to wipe the cheeks now covered in his come, as well as those hot Maori tats. "How're you doing in the dark, sexy?"

Still on all fours, Jeremy turned his head and sent Owen a shaky smile. "Ready to see my surprise. As soon as I can move my legs again."

Owen bent down to kiss his hip then pushed himself to his feet, helping Jeremy up and kissing him gently on the lips. "You can lean on me."

"Trust me, I plan to."

When he looked over at the cabin he'd parked their rental car next to, Owen finally got his first clear-headed glimpse at what he'd only seen online—and cringed. The picture had been an evil lie. He'd thought they were going to a beautiful lodge with two stories, a deck with an outdoor kitchen—the works.

Reality was *nothing* like the picture. It was the set of one of those campground horror movies, where the first people to have sex got axed. Luckily they'd nipped that myth in the bud before the sunset.

Fuck.

Take him to some romantic getaway where none of our relatives or his friends from the convention can get ahold of him, his cousin Brady had suggested. Of course, that was during the Great Rumming of 2015, when they'd both drunk too much and Brady had spouted all kinds of relationship advice he was in no way qualified to give.

Owen had rolled his eyes through most of it, but when he woke up with a mild headache the next morning, he couldn't get Brady's words out of his head.

You're a Finn. We go all in or not at all.

That was how Owen had always tried to live. If he wanted something, he went after it. When he'd made up his mind that he wanted Jeremy, he'd knocked over every obstacle Jeremy threw in his path and ignored every good reason why they shouldn't be together, to get him.

Of course, communication had never been one of his talents, and his actions didn't always go over well with the man he loved.

He still remembered showing up late at the lake house with a *U-Haul* full of his things and realizing that

Jeremy had thought they were over. He'd had no idea that Owen loved him, because Owen hadn't bothered to say out loud what seemed so fucking obvious. What he thought Jeremy should've already known.

It still wasn't easy for Owen to talk about feelings that weren't lust and love. About needs that weren't the basics like sex and hunger. Or sleep and sex. But he'd been trying...until he'd started seeing signs that their relationship was in trouble.

Owen tightened his arm reflexively around Jeremy's waist. He couldn't lose him. He refused to let it happen. He wasn't going to let some coffee table book photographer swoop in and steal his happiness.

Jeremy was his. And Brady was right, Owen had wanted to propose the second his shamrock lamp found its new home in the guest room instead of the trash. Even before that, if he was honest with himself.

When he'd thought about it, Brady's suggestion had seemed like the perfect solution. A getaway. Just the two of them with no interruptions for two weeks. No houseguest who wouldn't leave. No wedding to plan for Stephen and Tasha or baby to shop for. No conventions, and no phone calls from other men that Jeremy had to take outside. Not even Badass, who was just too damn cute not to be an attention-stealer.

He could shout his love from the damn rooftops, and he would, but before he slapped a bumper sticker on their truck that showed his true colors to the world, he had to make sure Jeremy was tied down. In every possible sense.

So he'd scheduled his vacation, spent the next few days relegating his duties at the construction company and then packed their bags. He hadn't *communicated* to Jeremy where they were going, and he'd hidden his phone. He'd wanted the cabin to be a romantic surprise.

Well, he'd gotten the surprise part right anyway.

Sighing, Owen released Jeremy and reached up to remove his blindfold. "Surprise."

He watched closely as Jeremy blinked, getting used to the sunlight, and knew the moment his eyes finally landed on the cabin. "Wow."

Fuck, he *sucked* at romance. "We don't have to stay…"

"No," Jeremy soothed, reaching down to pull his jeans up over his ass. "It isn't that bad at all. It has character."

Owen stared at him and Jeremy chuckled. "Okay it looks like a shithole, but it might be better inside. How did you find this place?"

"Online. I should have checked for reviews." Owen followed him up the rickety steps to the faded gray cabin. He should also have been suspicious when the deposit was so affordable. "They said the key would be under the—"

"It's open," Jeremy said as he disappeared inside.

"Son of a bitch." Owen looked for the welcome mat that was supposed to have his receipt and a spare key. Nothing but rotting wood. "Great."

"Hey, there's running water."

Jeremy's call from inside the cabin pulled him in against his will. He went directly to the light switched and flipped it up. Thank God. "We've got electricity too."

Strong arms wrapped around his waist and he tilted his head so Jeremy could kiss his neck. "You might not believe me, but I love this surprise, Owen. Two weeks of no distractions? Just you and me with nothing to do but each other? Sounds like heaven to me."

Owen felt a grumpy growl forming in his chest. Apparently, Heaven was a one-room cabin with a large copper bathtub…and no furniture.

Surprise.

JEREMY

Jeremy knew Owen was miserable, but he wasn't sure what to do about it. From what he'd said before he went outside to "take a look around," they were a half hour away from a super Walmart and a Loews, but he hadn't seen a single hotel. He'd picked this place in the middle of nowhere, and now he was definitely regretting it.

It did have a *The Hills Have Eyes* kind of vibe to it, but Jeremy wasn't too focused on that. He was still recovering from Owen's "Welcome to our vacation" sex and enjoying the fact that he'd put this together in the first place.

Owen fucking Finn, the gorgeous, insatiable couch potato who believed there was no place like home, had

261

planned a two-week vacation. Their first trip as a couple, and close enough to their one year anniversary to be called romantic.

"I'll be damned," Jeremy huffed out, smiling as he cleaned up dinner.

According to Owen, the fridge was supposed to be stocked—and it was. With frozen dinners and little else. When they'd made that discovery, they'd also seen a note stuck to the freezer that made Owen swear softly. "We're in the right place, damn it. This says, 'We hope you enjoy your stay, Owen and...Jenny.'" They'd chuckled, popped two Hungry Man's in the oven and then eaten on the floor in silence.

Jeremy glanced over at the focal point of the room. That was one giant bathtub. Old fashioned, saloon-style and sturdy. He had a feeling it was just what the doctor ordered to improve Owen's mood. He looked for something to wipe it down and got to work.

By the time Owen had come back in, the scalding-hot water was filling the tub and Jeremy had everything ready.

"I didn't see anyone creeping around with bloody machetes, but there's a workshop in the back," Owen started as soon as he came in. "A sawhorse and—what are you doing?"

He let Owen's gaze linger over his naked body before turning to bend over and shut off the water. "I think we could both use a bath, don't you? If you take off your clothes and join me, I might even scrub your back."

Owen eyed him suspiciously. "Are you sure it's—"

"And fuck you."

"I'm in." Owen kicked off his boots, and shucked his jeans with such swift expertise that Jeremy had to laugh.

"You *are* a sex addict."

Owen was in front of him, pulling him closer with firm hands on his hips before he could finish his sentence. "That's not a nice thing to say, *Jenny*."

"Payback is a bitch, Finn. Get in the tub."

Jeremy studied the man who'd changed his life a year ago, the man who'd been his straight best friend for two decades before deciding he wanted to see how the other half lived.

Owen's dark blond hair, bleached golden by the sun from his day job, was a little longer than it had been the first time Jeremy had run his fingers through it, and the lines around his crystal blue eyes were a little deeper lately—from whatever he'd had on his mind. But he was still the sexiest man in any room. Or plane.

Jeremy shook his head ruefully. He wasn't exaggerating about that stewardess. She's been on Owen since takeoff, so tenacious he wouldn't be surprised if she'd slipped her phone number into his man's pocket, and Owen hadn't told him because he didn't think it mattered.

It took some getting used to, being in a relationship with someone who seemed to emit sexual pheromones. If Owen hadn't made sure the both of them went to bed too exhausted to move every night for the last year, Jeremy would be insecure.

But he wasn't. Owen told him he loved him every day and rarely gave him room to doubt that he was happy. Until recently.

Shaking off his worry, Jeremy followed Owen into the bathtub and they splashed and swore, squeaking around in the tub and laughing together until they found the right fit.

Reaching for his soap on the chair he'd pushed beside the tub, he handed it to Owen before leaning back on his side of the curved copper. "All the comforts of home."

Owen snorted. "I'm not sure where you've been living, Porter, but I'll admit, any tub that can fit two men over six feet tall is worthy of praise."

"We should get one just like it," Jeremy said casually. "Think of the possibilities."

Blue eyes darkened with interest and arousal. "Believe me, I'm thinking."

"Give me that." Jeremy took the soap and lathered his hands, washing himself and trying to ignore Owen's long, lean legs resting over his.

Wash first, then fun. "Did you say Tanaka took Brady home the other night?"

"He did. When Brady called me back the next morning he said Ken had hired him to help with a job. He sounded distracted, but it's more likely he was hung over. The Finn giant put away most of the rum in the bar."

Frowning, Jeremy asked, "Do you think he's okay? Should we feel like shit?"

"He's fine," Owen said, shaking his head. "I promise you, he was ready for the change."

Jeremy knew some of the guilt was his own baggage, hating the idea that anyone would feel unwanted in his home after what his parents had done to him. But Brady was more fragile than the other Finns knew. He couldn't sleep. He could never relax unless he was doing something for someone else—almost to a penance level.

He was running from some inner demons, and he'd managed to put a few of them to rest in their guestroom.

Owen was watching him. "You know I didn't kick him out. I love that guy and he fixed our roof. But you have to admit the last few days have been nice. Just the two of us again."

Jeremy smiled. "You're just happy to get your high score back."

"I'm happy because our Marine has gone without for at least eight months and Tanaka clearly has a hardcore case of lust. Hopefully before the job is done, he'll tie my cousin down and help him release all that pent up sexual energy."

"Even drunk, I can't see Brady agreeing to that." Brady couldn't have made himself clearer every time the topic came up. Kink was *not* his thing.

But then, Jeremy had thought the same thing. Before Owen.

Jeremy dropped his hands to Owen's legs, caressing them beneath the water. "Feeling better?"

Owen let his head fall back with a groan and slid down the side of the tub just enough to dip his hair into the warm water. He raised back up and swiped away the rivulets running down his face. "God, that's good. But no. I have crashed and burned in the planning-trips department. Fuck vacations. As soon as you stop doing that I'm going to dig my phone out of hiding and change our flight. We'll get home, order a pizza, play a little Swords…and do what comes naturally."

His words didn't match his tone. He sounded defeated. It wasn't like Owen at all. Easygoing and full-steam-ahead—that was Owen. Jeremy didn't like how worried that made him. What the hell was going on with his Finn?

Jeremy gripped Owen's thighs and pulled him onto his lap, heedless of the splashing water. "No."

"Wha—Jeremy what are you doing?"

"We're not going anywhere. Not for the next two weeks."

Owen looked at him as if he'd lost his mind. "Babe, look around. No bed, no couch, no radio or television. All we have here are frozen dinners, a tub and a cabin that could fall down around us at any moment. It's my fault, and I'll accept the blame, but those are the facts. Why in God's name would we want to stay?"

Jeremy reached up and dragged Owen's head down for a passionate kiss without answering. Their moans of desire mingled as they ate at each other's mouths, tongues dueling and tangling, teeth scraping lips and biting hungrily.

Sliding his large hand around Owen's erection, Jeremy stroked it the way he knew Owen could never resist. He loved the sounds he was making. Loved how quickly he could drive him wild.

Owen turned his head, panting. "Fuck, Jeremy. You know I can't think when you do that."

He was counting on it. "I want you on your knees, hands on the edge of the tub," he ordered roughly. "You don't have to think at all. Just do it for me."

Owen shuddered and lifted himself off Jeremy's lap, splashing more water onto the floor as he turned and positioned himself.

Jeremy got to his knees behind him. "That's exactly what I wanted."

He reached for the bottle of lube they'd brought with them and opened the cap, taking his time. He drizzled some on his erection and let more drip between the cheeks of Owen's ass.

"I remember the first time I got inside you," he murmured. "You were begging me, ordering me to take you, despite your virgin ass. I was so fucking turned on. And so worried I'd hurt you."

"You didn't," Owen rasped. "Okay, you did, but in the best fucking way. You filled me with that big fat cock and turned me into an addict."

"I'm the one who's addicted," Jeremy countered, pressing the pads of his fingers against Owen's tight ass. "That's why I let you take me blindfolded in the dirt. Why I beg for that damn paddle of yours. Why my mouth waters every time I see your delicious dick."

Owen moaned when Jeremy pushed two fingers inside his snug hole.

"Yes." He pushed back, his hands tight on the tub's edge. "I can give it to you right now, Jeremy. I love it when you suck me off. I love fucking that hot mouth. I want it all the time."

He did. In alleys and office buildings, the dock on the lake, and once in a damn movie theater. And Jeremy could never resist him. He'd dropped to his knees and take him anytime he asked. He thought about the airplane, trying to remember if that was the first time he'd turned him down.

"You want me to stop this so I can taste you instead?" Jeremy thrust his fingers deeper, curling them until Owen let out a soft cry.

"*No.* Fuck, no. Don't stop. You know what I want."

"You want this all the time too, don't you? You like your handcuffs and toys but you fucking *love* having me inside you."

"Yes, damn it. You know I do," Owen admitted raggedly. "Please, Jeremy. Don't tease me."

Jeremy was too turned on for that. Something about this stark place made him feel wilder than usual. More aggressive. "I hope you're ready for me."

He guided his thick shaft slowly inside, groaning when Owen's ass closed around him like a hungry fist. It didn't matter how many times he'd had him, this first stretch always brought him right up to the edge. "God, Owen."

"Yes," Owen gasped. "*More*."

"Don't worry, you're getting everything," Jeremy ground out, pressing his hips forward. "Every fucking inch."

"Put up or shut up."

Jeremy tightened his hands on Owen's hips and dragged him back onto his shaft with his next thrust, making both of them groan. "Don't push," he warned. "I'm feeling some serious primal urges here."

"Primal?" Owen shivered, looking over his shoulder, water dripping from his hair.

Jeremy could feel the sharp edge to his smile. "This place makes me want to do things to you. Bad things to this ass." He thrust more forcefully, nearly all the way in, and they both inhaled sharply.

"Oh, you bastard," Owen moaned. "You manipulative, tricky, ba—"

Jeremy dragged him completely onto his cock, his hips pressed against Owen's ass as the man beneath him struggled to catch his breath. Fuck, that was good. He leaned forward until his chest was pressed to Owen's back, one arm wrapped his waist and the other across his shoulders and chest, holding him still.

Slow, shallow thrusts at first, then longer strokes, just the way he liked it. The way they both loved it. Jeremy slid his hand down Owen's tight abdomen, and then further.

"I think you like that idea," he whispered, rocking his hips forward as he stroked Owen's cock. "I think you want me like this. Wild for you. Only you, with no one to stop me from giving you what your ass is begging for."

He was shameless. But Owen always brought this out in him.

"*Motherfuck*—yes. I want it. You're in me so deep

and I still want more. I'll always... *Don't stop.*"

Jeremy was too far gone to play now. He had to have him. Had to come inside him and hear his cries. He started an unforgiving rhythm that made Owen shout his name. "Love fucking you, baby. Love you so much. Love how this tight ass takes me."

The sounds of slapping skin and sloshing water couldn't drown out Owen's pleasure. "*God!* Fucking me so good I can't breathe. Fuck, it's so good."

Jeremy felt Owen's climax in his hand and then he was joining him, shuddering as the waves crashed over his body. Owen. Always Owen.

Love you so much.

Owen

"Son of a bitch." Owen shoved his injured thumb in his mouth and glared at the offending hammer.

It was his own fault. He'd been distracted all morning. Stuck in a loop he couldn't get out of. Probably because it was day ten of their fourteen-day vacation and he still hadn't brought up the subject of his future with Jeremy. Mainly that he wanted one, and he wanted it on official, legally binding documents.

He'll say yes.

Fuck Brady anyway for putting that in his head. It had sounded great at first. Exactly what he'd wanted to hear. But the longer he waited, the more he put it off, the more it sounded like a curse. Something he was going to miss because he was a tool who couldn't just fucking ask one simple question.

What was stopping him? The issues his cousin had brought up—Owen's inability to admit he was gay, and his surprise that some people, both gay and straight, were not as thrilled with his happiness as his family had been?

Well, fuck them anyway. He didn't need people like that in his life.

It bothered him that people could be that ignorant, so he tried to avoid the subject altogether. But Brady told him it upset Jeremy. Made him wonder if Owen was in it for the long haul. And that was unacceptable.

He wasn't as worried about people giving him the side eye as he was about Jeremy's schedule the last few months. Between babysitting for Seamus, planning Tasha's wedding and all his recent "work" phone calls, Owen felt like he was being avoided. Like Jeremy was pulling away.

Not during sex. Sex had never been their problem. But he couldn't shake his fear that he could lose Jeremy and he didn't know how to stop it from happening.

He would do whatever it took, though. He would even let Jeremy drive him up the wall with his version of a romantic vacation.

The first morning they woke up on a pile of their own clothes, Owen had cursed the crick in his neck, forgotten about how hard Jeremy had ridden him the night before and started to look for his phone.

But Jeremy had stopped him with a massage that brought him to his knees and, before he knew it, they were back on the floor pumping their way to climax inside each other's mouths. While he was still recovering, Jeremy had suggested a shopping trip.

Since it was almost physically impossible for Owen to say no to him in that state, Owen had slipped on his jeans and grabbed his keys.

What Jeremy proposed in the car had sounded like an insane idea. A waste of vacation time and money. But as he spoke, he'd unzipped Owen's jeans and fondled him until he'd had to pull over so he wouldn't drive into a tree.

The same tree he leaned against while Jeremy knelt by the side of the road and sucked his cock until he came.

Jeremy Porter was a sneaky bastard, and he knew exactly what he was doing. He'd done everything but bend him over in the check-out line to distract him, and Owen was loving letting him but now he'd finally decided to give in. If this was what Jeremy wanted, what would make him happy, then damn it, that's what they were going to do.

Wouldn't the owners of the scary shack be surprised when they came back to find a real live cabin with a new paint job, a deck and a few necessary pieces of furniture?

He pulled his thumb out of his mouth and looked at the red appendage. He'd done a lot of complaining those first few days, most of it silent so Jeremy wouldn't stop the full-body massages he was getting so used to. But Owen had to admit things were starting to take shape. He'd even gotten a welcome mat for the front door, after he'd fixed those stairs.

For his part, Jeremy seemed to be having a great time. He told Owen that it felt like they were creating something together, with Owen building things that he could help design and paint.

He was in love with an artist. A geek with broad shoulders, muscles for miles, a porn-sized cock and crazy ideas.

His only comfort was that even though they might be working on the cabin during the day, at night—and sometimes in the morning and on breaks in the afternoon—they were busy doing other things.

Being topped hadn't been in Owen's getaway plans. In fact he'd been imagining keeping Jeremy tied down for two weeks until he submitted to Owen's true purpose—proposing. But he couldn't find it in him to be sorry.

Jeremy's sexual aggression had been his hottest wet dream come to life. *He'd* been the one tied up. He'd been the one begging for more when Jeremy took him up against the wall, his teeth digging into Owen's neck.

Owen lifted his hand to the mark there, wondering how shocked the people who knew him from the BDSM club would be to hear about all the things he'd been willing, even eager, to do for Jeremy each night.

Master Finn, indeed.

He wasn't that worried. He knew who he was and he'd accepted a while ago that what he had with Jeremy was unique. He didn't know anyone else like them, anyone else who had what they had. They had a chemistry that burned so hot it seemed as if it would never burn out. But they also had a true, long-lasting friendship.

Before they'd started having sex, for all of his adult life, Jeremy was the person Owen had turned to when he needed advice. When he just needed to be himself.

Jeremy was his go-to guy. Even before they'd fallen in love, he'd always been his. After? Well, this year had been the best of his life.

Before Jeremy started pulling away, everything had been perfect.

They'd gotten it back in the last ten days. Their connection. Their ability to just enjoy each other's company in between dirty fucking interludes of bliss. That was worth a little hammer to the thumb.

He felt it throb when he thought about it and decided to go inside for a cold beer and a break. When he left earlier, Jeremy had been planning to paint so all the windows were open as he walked toward the front door. He stopped moving when he heard Jeremy's voice.

"I won't. I want to tell him, but I won't." *Pause.* "There's nothing to be nervous about, I promise." *Pause.* "I do too. Talk to you soon."

For a minute Owen saw red, and then it felt like someone had hammered one nail into his head and another in his heart. He almost staggered from the surprise. They'd had a deal—no distractions, and that included no phones. Owen had hidden the damn thing in the trunk of the car, but Jeremy had obviously found it.

I want to tell him, but I won't.

Was it the photographer he'd met at conference—
George something? The one who'd been calling at least
once a day since Jeremy got back? The one Jeremy
lowered his voice for and left the room to talk to,
sending irritated looks at Owen when he found him
trying to listen in?

Owen had looked up George's work online. Most of
it was ridiculous nerd porn. Models dressed in
sexualized versions of comic book superheroes and
villains, with a lot of gender reversal. He might have
found it interesting if George wasn't the asshole trying
to steal his man.

His picture and bio really stuck in Owen's craw. He
was a handsome, openly gay and unattached man with a
killer smile, a man who bore enough resemblance to a
movie star Jeremy thought was attractive to make Owen
nervous. He also had Maori tattoos like Jeremy's, only
on his arm.

This was the man calling Owen's lover. This man
who went to the same conventions, knew the same
people in the industry and made no bones about
embracing his sexuality.

George was a threat.

When Brady was still living with them, he'd told

Owen more than once that it was just work. Jeremy didn't do nine-to-five. He was an artist. He kept strange hours from home and the other people in his industry did as well. His cousin was adamant that Jeremy was not that type of guy.

He wasn't. Owen knew he wasn't. But that insecure asshole inside him added it to the top of the proof pile, telling him Jeremy wasn't as sure about their future as he seemed.

Ever heard of projecting, Numbnuts?

Fuck that bastard. He hadn't come out to the ass end of nowhere so that hot, gay, talented George could steal his man before he had the chance to tell him how he felt.

In a small quadrant in a deep, dark corner of his mind, a little voice told him he wasn't making any sense. That he should be more confident than ever that Jeremy was his. That he shouldn't fuck it all up by making a jackass out of himself and saying something he was going to regret.

Owen gave that little voice the finger and slammed open the door. "What the *hell*, Jeremy?"

Jeremy had turned toward him with a smile, yellow paint on his cheek and phone in his hand, but he froze when he saw Owen's face. "What's wrong?"

Without a word, Owen strode over to him, grabbed the phone and flung it out the window. Jeremy's eyes went wide and his lips parted.

Surprise, Owen thought sarcastically. "Strip and get on the bed." If Jeremy's eyes got any wider they'd pop out. "Jeremy, take off your clothes and get on the bed. I won't ask you again."

Owen took off his flannel shirt and t-shirt, heading to the sink without looking to see if Jeremy obeyed. He washed the sawdust off, ran his thumb under the cold water for a minute and then searched for a towel to dry off with while he looked around.

They'd done all this in ten days. The kitchen was a warm gold with white trim and homey-looking curtains. The refrigerator was full of actual food, including produce, and there was a small table and two chairs where Owen and Jeremy could have breakfast before they started their day.

In the main room they'd just refinished the wood and there was an affordable but comfortably wide couch, an area rug and a coffee table—Jeremy had forbidden a television. The rest of the cabin was taken up by that giant copper tub…and the bed.

Owen had insisted on the four-poster and high-end

mattress. The memory of that night on the floor was still too recent. He wanted something comfortable for his damn vacation.

The bed currently had another feature that drew Owen closer. Jeremy. Naked and kneeling. He looked more confused than guilty, but that wasn't going to change what had to happen.

Owen went to his gym bag in the corner of the room and brought it to the bed, setting it down beside Jeremy. He opened it and pulled out two thick lengths of corded rope, a butt plug, and the travel-sized flogger, making sure the kneeling man could see everything.

Jeremy inhaled at the sight and Owen wanted to smile, but his emotions were still too volatile. He was going to have to do this slowly. He needed to be in control of himself before he played his lover.

But that didn't mean he couldn't prep him now.

He slid one length of rope through his hand, knowing Jeremy was watching his every move. "Turn and face the wall."

"Owen, you—"

"The faster you do this, the sooner I'll let you speak."

Jeremy turned on the bed until he was facing the wall on his knees.

"Give me your wrist."

Jeremy lifted his arm and Owen made short work of forming a rope cuff and attaching it to the thick wooden post nearest the wall. After he tested its hold, he took the second bit of rope, walked to the other side of the bed and repeated the process.

Then he took a step back and stared. Jeremy's body always gave him so much pleasure. Just looking at him made Owen hard. *Happy.* It made Owen ache to think the sight could ever be taken away from him. It made him jealous and stupid and crazy.

He walked over to where Jeremy had left the lube and came back to the bed. Coating his fingers, he traced the Maori design, feeling the scar tissue on Jeremy's ass cheek. "You look like a captured warrior right now. I'd take a picture, but I left my phone turned off in the trunk."

The cheek flexed and Jeremy sighed. "Owen, if you'd let me tell you…"

Owen placed one knee on the bed and moved closer, slipping his fingers between Jeremy's firm cheeks and making him gasp.

"Why ruin this by giving in so easily?" Owen murmured, pushing through the tight ring of muscles with one finger and feeling the stretch. "I was thinking about the first time you did this to me in your shower. I was fucking begging for it. I know now I wasn't ready for it yet, but I'd have given anything, done anything, to have more. I was lost from the second you let me see you. Touch you."

He was lost before that, but he hadn't known it at the time.

Owen slid a second finger in to join the first and went deep, finding and massaging Jeremy's prostate. "Remember?"

"Oh God, Owen. Yes. *Fuck*, of course I remember." His head fell back. "Jesus, that's…"

Owen bit the inside of his cheek hard and dragged his hand back, removing his fingers, his touch. "It's not going to be as easy for you, Jeremy. I'm not as giving as you are and you're going to have to work for it."

JEREMY

The alarm clock he'd bought for the bedside table said it had been an hour.

An hour. He's been winding me up for an hour.

Jeremy knew he could have stopped Owen at any time. He had a safe word, and if that didn't work, he could have ripped these damn posts off the bed so they could talk about the stupid phone and Owen's reaction to it.

But he hadn't.

He wanted to say it was because he knew Owen was working something out, working up to a conversation that had been in the air for weeks. But the truth was baser. Simpler.

When Owen ordered him onto the bed, all Jeremy

had wanted to do was submit. He'd never been able to explain it. From that first experience with a paddle, he'd been a willing student. As much as he craved and loved taking Owen and claiming him, exploring his primal side, he needed this. It was one of the reasons he believed their sex was always so combustible. It was all need and no rules. A true partnership. They didn't have to want just one thing, be just one thing. To each other, they were the whole package.

This time Owen seemed determined to keep him on the ragged edge, waiting for a punishment that never came. The flogger still hadn't been touched since Owen set it beside him. It was more mind fuck than physical pain, which for Jeremy was always harder to endure.

At first, Owen had fingered his ass, stopping when Jeremy's hips started pushing back in need. He'd done it again, and again until Jeremy realized his true punishment. He was being denied orgasm.

His big body had shuddered when Owen spread his cheeks and circled his anus with his skilled tongue. He'd pushed it inside and moaned hungrily, giving Jeremy hope that we was losing control. But he hadn't. He'd stopped again and gotten off the bed, leaving Jeremy alone for five endless minutes only to come back and repeat the process.

The next time he joined Jeremy he'd played with his ass cheeks. Squeezing and spanking them, spreading them and massaging them. Then Owen's hands had traveled over his body, tracing every tattoo, testing every muscle before returning to his ass for a single sharp spank.

The last time, he'd inserted the butt plug—although *inserted* wasn't exactly the right word. He'd used it to fuck Jeremy with shallow thrusts until he was shaking. Moaning. Then he'd pushed it all the way in and left again.

And the whole time, Owen hadn't said a word, which was the biggest mind fuck of all. He loved saying things to drive Jeremy wild. Loved to give dirty running commentary while Jeremy fucked him. If Jeremy hadn't been so lost in the treatment his body was receiving, he would have started to worry.

The bed dipped and he tensed, knowing Owen was back for more. Owen's hand shook on the butt plug for a moment and then he tugged on it, not quite hard enough to pull it out. Another tease then.

Jeremy couldn't take any more. He struggled for breath and turned to look over his shoulder, and Owen's expression told him he was as bad off as he was. As needy.

"Owen, please."

Crystal blue eyes darkened when he saw Jeremy watching him. "Do you want me to stop?"

"I want *you*."

Pulling out the plug without argument, Owen placed it off to the side before climbing onto the bed behind him. Jeremy heard his zipper as he opened his jeans and his heart started to race. "Owen?"

"I'm giving you what you want." His voice was raw with arousal and he pressed his forehead on Jeremy's shoulder. "I need you."

"Yes," Jeremy gasped, breathless. "Take it. Whatever you need. Please, God, take it."

He gasped again when more cool lube slid between his cheeks. Owen spread them wide enough to sting and then he was in him, filling him without preamble. Without stopping.

Yes. Please don't stop.

Owen's chest was hot against his back, one hand strong on his hip while the other stroked the length of his painful erection. "Sorry," he whispered as he pumped deeper inside him. "I need you. Love you, baby. I'm sorry."

Why was he sorry?

"I love you too," Jeremy moaned. "You feel so good, Owen. Don't stop. *Please* don't stop again."

"Never," he growled, his pace faster as his cock filled him.

Fuck, yes. Fuck me. Don't stop fucking me. Love it so much. Need to come.

"You're so damn tight," Owen groaned. "I couldn't get enough. I'll never get enough."

Jeremy's arms ached from being held in the same position, his body on fire from prolonged frustration, but it was worth it. It was all worth it if Owen let him come. He was so close. "Please, Owen. Harder. Don't stop."

The hand on his erection tightened, pumping in time with his hips. *Harder. Faster, oh fuck, that was it. Almost. Almost there.* "Owen!"

The waves rushed in and covered him. Pulling him under in a climax so intense he nearly passed out. All he could do was feel. All he could feel was Owen. He needed Owen with him.

Owen stiffened behind him, shouting his name as he found his climax. Jeremy could feel Owen's release dripping down onto his ass cheeks and thighs as he pulled out. He smiled like an idiot, unable to stop himself. Relief and subspace combined to make him dizzy.

It took him a minute to realize his arms were free. Owen rubbed them more vigorously than he had to, making sure circulation returned. Jeremy was tingling all over so it must be working.

He heard bathwater running. Were they taking a bath?

Owen helped him off the bed and into the tub, though he didn't join him. Jeremy was still smiling, his eyes half closed as Owen caressed him with a washcloth. "That feels wonderful, Finn."

"I'm glad." His voice was tight. Upset?

Jeremy forced his eyes to open fully. "What is it?"

"I wasn't in the right headspace to tie you up. It was irresponsible. That's why we couldn't use the flogger. Are your arms okay?"

Jeremy lifted them up and wiggled his fingers. "I'm good. You're not. Why did you?"

"Why did I what?"

"Tie me up when you were in the wrong headspace?"

Owen looked down, watching the washcloth trace circles on Jeremy's chest. "Honest answer? When I came in I was angry. I wanted to argue with you. Talk. But somehow I ended up tying you to the bed and torturing the both of us for the better part of an hour. I couldn't seem to stop myself."

Sighing, Jeremy reached up to cover Owen's hand with his own. "I'm sorry I used the phone. I found it in the trunk when I was looking for something else and I thought I'd just check my messages and turn it off again."

Owen's hand tensed against his chest. "But you didn't."

"No." Jeremy's brow furrowed. "What is going on in that head of yours?"

"Who was on the phone, Jeremy?"

The question had a jealous edge. But that didn't make any sense. Owen wasn't the insecure mess in this relationship. He was confident. He took what he wanted and he always wanted Jeremy. Worrying about sexy stewardesses and handsome bisexuals who wanted a piece of one sexy alpha owner of Finn Construction was Jeremy's job.

"Who?" Owen repeated.

"Tasha. Her message sounded upset so I called."

Owen looked surprised but still miserable. "She has a

husband who worships the ground she walks on and caters to her every whim. You'd think she could go a day without talking to you."

"You'd think it if you hadn't known us for twenty years, but you have so there's no excuse. We *always* talk. Though, to be fair to her, she hadn't left a single message since I sent her that video at the airport. I think she was feeling anxious and had no one else to talk to."

Worry replaced irritation. "Is she okay? Is it the baby? I'm her friend and brother-in-law—what weren't you supposed to tell me?"

"I wasn't supposed to tell *Stephen* that the radiologist saw something in her last ultrasound and wanted her to come back today for another look." Jeremy reached up to caress Owen's jaw. "I'm sure it's nothing, but she's having her first baby at thirty-five, so they're covering all the bases."

He waited until Owen leaned into his hand to ask, "What is it, Owen? I thought you'd been feeling better since we got here."

"Better?"

Jeremy lifted his eyebrow. "Yes, better. You think I don't know you, Owen Finn? I've known you most of my life and I know that you haven't been yourself for the last few months. Is it your parents? Because they're both doing better now. Or did something else happen at work?"

He hoped someone else hadn't quit because they'd found out Owen was with Jeremy. It had been hard for him to hold a carefree smile in place when he'd found out about that.

Owen shook his head. "Neither. Who's George?"

"George?" Jeremy's surprise turned into suspicion. "Did I tell you his name?"

"You haven't told me much."

He couldn't help it. He started to laugh. "Jesus, you crack me up."

"I'm serious, Jeremy. I want to know who this George is and why he thinks calling you every damn day is okay with me."

"You *are* serious." Jeremy sighed again, lifting himself out of the tub and walking across the room, heedless of his dripping body. "George is a friend who makes superhero coffee table books and goes to conventions to hunt for models."

"I know that. Did he want you to model?"

"No, but I would if he asked. I'd make you do it too." Ignoring Owen's growl, Jeremy lifted one wet hand as he reached under the bed for his suitcase. "I get it. You're scary jealous guy now. Or you're having pizza withdrawals, which I wouldn't rule out."

He knew it was in here somewhere... There. He picked up the box wrapped in plain brown paper and held it up triumphantly. "Bring me a towel so I don't get our new couch all wet."

Maybe he should be angry or insulted that Owen didn't trust him. Maybe he was still high on endorphins and warm from the bath and he'd get pissed later. Or maybe he just loved the man and knew him well enough to realize there was more going on than jealousy over his phone time with Tasha and George. By taking his reasons for being jealous off the table, Jeremy hoped he'd tell him what it was.

After Owen had laid a towel on the couch, Jeremy sat down and handed him the box. "This is for you." He laughed at Owen's expression. "It isn't a bomb. Open it."

Owen started to unwrap it and Jeremy inwardly crossed his fingers that he'd like it. "It's chock-full of cheese, but I did it for our anniversary and your birthday," he murmured softly.

When Owen opened the box and saw the large,

leather-bound book and the golden engraving on the cover, he smiled.

"The Finn Factor: A Family Album," he read out loud before looking up at Jeremy, still smiling but obviously a bit confused.

"Open it," Jeremy urged him.

As Owen began to turn the pages, Jeremy spoke. "I started making sketches of your family last summer," he reminded him. "I wanted to capture all of them, and it was a way to draw something other than our favorite vigilante demon. As much as I love him, he gets monotonous."

Owen turned a page, and on one side Jeremy saw the sketch he'd done of Jennifer Finn fishing on the dock— on the other was a full color drawing of her as a superhero. She was smiling Little Finn's mischievous smile as she dragged a fresh catch of men behind her in a fishing net. Owen laughed softly.

"I think it really captures her essence," Jeremy chuckled. "Anyway I didn't know how to put something like this together, so George agreed to help me organize the artists. We called several of my fellow graphic artists and asked them each to make one superhero based on my sketches and a list of particular personality quirks. In this case, two, because I couldn't separate your parents, even in art."

Owen was touching Jeremy's sketches of Ellen and Shawn as he glanced over at the rendering of them as Greek gods, clinging to each other and looking down at all their super-children with pride and love in their eyes.

"I like that," he murmured.

They both cracked up when they saw Seamus standing behind a bar, dressed head to toe in dented armor as a swarm of children climbed on his shoulders. "Poor Seamus," Owen wheezed, wiping his eyes from laughter. "Even his superhero needs an adult vacation."

Tasha and Stephen were next. Senator Finn was pulling open his suit to reveal a letter S on his chest, and Tasha looked stunning in a slinky black cat suit, wielding a whip in one hand, and a chocolate cake in the other.

"S&M," Owen snorted. "They'll love it."

Jeremy knew what came next, watching as he turned page after page of sketches, all of them of Owen. Owen sleeping, laughing, playing with his nephews or Badass. Owen talking quietly with his mother at the hospital.

"I might have the hots for this subject," Jeremy said. It was true. Once he'd started drawing Owen, he couldn't seem to stop.

The last page was his superhero. "You drew this," he said without question.

"I did."

Owen was a stunning blond superhero in tights with a tool belt around his waist and a shamrock glowing on his chest. He had a giant hammer in his hand as he hovered over the lake, building a stairway up to the heavens. On the dock below, Jeremy had drawn himself holding a pizza box for the superhero, with Badass looking up, both of them cheering Owen on.

He stared at it for a long time then closed the book, tracing the letters with his fingers. "This is..." he started. "Thank you."

"Thank George," Jeremy insisted. "Seriously, he pushed everyone to get the job done in time. I'm just glad it arrived before we left on our surprise getaway."

"I will thank George profusely," Owen promised him, shaking his head. "Jeremy, I don't even know how to start apologizing for being such an asshole. I just thought— Hell, I wasn't thinking. Things have been so fucking perfect here and then I had to ruin it over a phone call."

"You didn't ruin anything. I just wish you'd tell me

what's really wrong."

Owen opened his mouth, hesitated, then shook his head again. "Can we talk about it later?"

"Fine. You get one free pass because of this vacation." Jeremy looked around the cabin. "I almost wish we didn't have to leave. I love it here. I can't believe we did all this in less than two weeks."

"You might be able to talk me into staying longer with a few more massages and a lifetime of sexual favors." Owen smiled. "But you know I need a big screen and delivery pizza to survive."

Jeremy couldn't deny it. "I know. And you have that business to run. I guess we'll have to go back to the real world and stop pretending we're the only people on Earth."

"Back to the daily grind," Owen agreed.

"Back to family errands and emergency phone calls." Jeremy smiled. "That is, if Master Finn lets me have my phone back."

Owen seemed to be considering it. "Maybe I can hide your phone one weekend a month?"

"Deal."

Owen's expression was sincere. "I love this book, Jeremy. This is the best present anyone's ever given me."

He tangled his hands in Jeremy's hair and tugged him closer, whispering, "Except for that one you got me last year."

OWEN

Thank God for Seamus.

He'd been sending Owen texts all evening, keeping him up to date on what was going on. He'd managed to bring the whole family together for a surprise Finn Again, and filled the pub with strangers, regulars and people from Owen's club by offering free food and drink.

He'd also gotten everyone matching Finn Club t-shirts.

Owen owed his brother big time.

"It's crowded," Jeremy said as they parked on a side street. "Seamus must be swamped. I hope he called in some help."

Owen took his hand. "If he didn't, we can help him

out after we talk to Solomon and James."

Jeremy frowned. "Did they give you details when they called? Is Brady okay? It must be serious if Solomon wants to see us in person."

It *was* serious, but it didn't have anything to do with Brady.

It was a surprise party for Jeremy. His anniversary present. Owen had something to say, something Jeremy deserved to hear, and he needed the biggest audience he could round up to witness it.

He'd been a fucking idiot. Jealous and insecure. The reasons he had for taking Jeremy away, all his plans to *tie him down*, seemed so ridiculous now. Jeremy had never been pulling away—he'd been doing what he'd always done. Taking care of Tasha, taking care of Brady, taking care of Owen's parents and Badass and, most of all, taking care of him.

It had all been in Owen's head. His fears. His problem that needed to be fixed.

That book had been the punch in the gut he'd needed. Seeing his family, seeing *himself* through Jeremy's eyes, had woken him up. Reminded him how well Jeremy knew him. How much he was loved.

Why he never had to worry about Jeremy walking

away.

The stone-faced James was standing by the front door of the pub, watching them approach. "We've been waiting for you." He tilted his head toward the sound of cheers and laughter. "Solomon's inside."

"This might not be the best place to talk about Brady," Jeremy said when they opened the door and the noise hit them both in a wave. "Wait, why is Little Finn here? And Tasha? Did we miss an invitation?"

Jeremy let go of his hand and slowed his steps so they weren't walking side by side. Owen had done that to him, he knew—made it their habit not to be too public with their affection in front of strangers. God, he deserved the flogger. And not in a good way.

When Seamus saw them and gave Owen the thumbs up, Owen nodded.

Seamus raised his glass and started a chain reaction of spoons tapping beer bottles, the crowd quieting as they looked toward him expectantly.

"That something special I've been telling you about has arrived. A lot of you know my brother Owen." Several tables cheered loudly. "Well, he's got something to say, so give him a round of applause so he can get to it."

Owen couldn't look at Jeremy. Not yet.

One of the members of the band brought Seamus a microphone and he held it out, looking into Owen's eyes with a proud smile. "Owen?"

There was nothing he could do about the mutant butterflies in his stomach. If he made a jackass out of himself, so be it. This was too important. Jeremy was too important.

He walked up and took the microphone, then turned to see all those faces staring at him expectantly. Some were familiar, some weren't, but there was only one that mattered. Jeremy. He was looking a little pale, and Solomon had a hand on his shoulder. He sent Owen a frowning nod of encouragement.

He should have rehearsed this.

"Is Brady Finn here?"

"I am, Owen. How was your vacation?" Brady was sitting close to Ken Tanaka, a confused smile on his face.

"Good. Thanks for asking." Owen slipped one hand in his jeans pocket and spoke into the microphone. "Brady gave me some good advice a few weeks ago—"

"During the Great Rumming of 2015!" Tanaka called out, making the crowd laugh.

"Yes. Rum was involved. But I remembered everything he said and his words stuck with me. See, I've been in a serious relationship for about a year now, and I've never been happier, but there were a few things I couldn't face. Refused to face. Obstacles I'd put in my own path out of fear or habit, I don't fucking know. Basically I was a dumbass."

"What else is new?" Someone from the club called out, making Owen smile.

He snared Jeremy's gaze again. "This is only going to work if you come up and stand beside me."

It was clear Jeremy didn't want to. That he still wasn't sure what was going on. Solomon nudged him and he moved forward slowly, his face so expressive Owen could practically see the gears turning in his mind.

He reached out and took Jeremy's hand, tangling their fingers together. The crowd welcomed Jeremy with claps and cheers.

"He's handsome isn't he?" Owen winked, relaxing as soon as Jeremy was touching him. "I'm a lucky man. You have no idea *how* lucky."

Jeremy squeezed his hand in warning.

"Don't worry, I won't go into intimate details." He glanced back at his audience. "But seriously? *Huge* amount of luck."

The crowd guffawed and Jeremy leaned closer. "What the hell are you doing?"

"Being romantic and impulsive?" He raised his voice. "Tonight my brother Seamus threw this party at my request because there's something I want to say...and something I want to ask."

The patrons caught the hint, a hush falling over the crowd. This was it. Now or never.

"The first thing I need to say is I hate labels." When Brady and Seamus groaned, Owen said, "I'm sorry, but that's never going to change. I don't think what you are or what your sexuality is matters nearly as much as *who* you love and *how* you love."

He turned toward Jeremy, still holding his hand. "You're who I love, Jeremy Porter. And you teach me every day how to do it right. And because of that, I can say what Brady and my sister and everyone who knows me has been wanting me to admit out loud for a year now. Are you all listening?"

"Say it already!"

"Loud and proud!"

Owen chuckled and raised his voice. "I. Am. Gay."

Brady whooped and Owen's father laughed as his

mother leaned against him, clutching a handkerchief to wipe her tears.

Then Owen got down on one knee and several people gasped. "But only for you, Jeremy. You're the only man I've ever wanted. The only man I love. I've never had someone mean this much to me. So much I can't imagine walking through this world without you beside me. It made me crazy there for a while, worrying that what we had was too good and I was bound to fuck it all up."

He shrugged and smiled. "But I realized the other day that it's pointless to worry about something that's inevitable. I will fuck it up. I'll make a mess of things and steamroll over your plans. We'll argue, and I'll get jealous when you spend too much time away from me." He tightened his grip on Jeremy's hand. "But we'll also make up, laugh, and make a home out of the scariest fucking vacation cabin in the world."

He hoped Jeremy meant it when he said he liked that cabin, since he'd bought the damn thing yesterday. They'd made it together. It belonged to them now.

"It *will* happen, all of it, because that's life. And I want that life. I want to live every day of that life with you. I love you, Jeremy Porter. Will marry me?"

The pub got so loud that he wouldn't have been able to hear Jeremy even if he answered.

He lowered the microphone and got to his feet, pulling Jeremy closer. "Surprise," he said into his ear. "What do you say?"

Jeremy cupped Owen's jaw and stared at him as if memorizing every detail of his face. "As if you didn't know."

He kissed Owen and Owen groaned against his lips, only pulling back long enough to ask, "I think I kicked that proposal's ass, don't you?"

"Cocky bastard," Jeremy murmured, kissing him again.

Owen was a lucky man.

Everyone seemed to come up all at once, pulling them apart to hug them and offer their congratulations. Owen was over the moon. He'd said yes. Jeremy had said yes. There was nothing left to do but spend the rest of his life being blissfully content.

He turned at a tap on his shoulder and found Jeremy behind him. Owen smiled, a little tipsy and a lot happy. "Hey there."

Jeremy was grinning, his eyes sparkling when he pulled Owen's head down to whisper in his ear, "Out back. Now. I want to say yes again…on *my* knees."

"I'll follow you," he whispered back, watching Jeremy's wide frame part the crowd.

Hell yes, he was lucky. But he was a Finn. *All in or not at all.*

Look for Little Finn's (Jen's) story in ***Ravenous*** and
A Curious Wedding: An Owen and Jeremy quickie
Both Coming Soon!

THANKS FOR READING!

I truly hope you enjoyed this book. If so, please leave a review and tell your friends. Word of mouth and online reviews are immensely helpful to authors and greatly appreciated.

To keep up with all the latest news about RG's books, release info, exclusive excerpts and more, check out her website RGAlexander.com. Stop by her group blog, Smutketeers.com to enter the frequent *contests* and *free book giveaways* each month.

Friend me on **Facebook**
https://www.facebook.com/RGAlexander.RachelGrace
to join **The Brass Chattery**
https://www.facebook.com/groups/292493407577385/
for contests, and smutty fun.

CHECK OUT *Curious*,
BOOK 1 OF THE FINN FACTOR SERIES

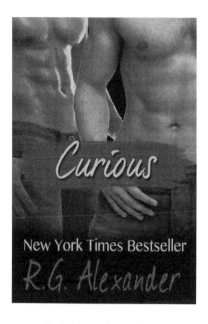

*"Everyone go buy the f***ing thing. Curious. Go now."* tweet
by author of Love Lessons,
Heidi Cullinan

*"When I got to the end of this book, I wanted to start over…
RG Alexander is one hell of an author!"*
USA Today bestselling **Bianca Sommerland**,
author of Iron Cross, the Dartmouth Cobras

Are you Curious?

Jeremy Porter is. Though the bisexual comic book artist
has known Owen Finn for most of his life—long enough
to know that he is terminally straight—he can't help but
imagine what things would be like if he weren't.

Owen is far from vanilla—as a dominant in the local fetish community, he sees as much action as Jeremy does. Lately even more.

Since Jeremy isn't into collars and Owen isn't into men, it seems like his fantasies will remain just that forever...until one night when Owen gets curious.

Warning: **READ THIS!** Contains explicit m/m nookie. A lot of it. Very detailed. Two men getting kinky, talking dirty and doing the horizontal mambo. Are you reading this? Do you see them on the cover? Guy parts will touch. You have been warned.

Available Now!
www.RGAlexander.com

The Finn Factor Series
(for the reader who enjoys variety)
Book 1: *Curious* (m/m)
Book 2: *Scandalous* (m/f)
Book 3: *Dangerous* (m/m)
Book 4: *Ravenous* (m/f/m)
Book 5: *Shameless* (?)

Big Bad John
Bigger in Texas series, Book One

Available Now!
www.RGAlexander.com

Kinda broad at the shoulder and narrow at the hip…

Trudy Adams never planned on going home again. Not to that sleepy little Texas town where everyone knew her business and thought she was trouble. She ran away to California years ago, and now, after what has felt like a lifetime of struggling, her lucky break might finally be around the corner.

And then she got that email.

John Brown has been waiting patiently for Trudy to return, but his patience has run out. He's had years to think about all the things he wants to do to her, and he's willing to use her concern for her brother, her desire to help her best friend get her story, and every kinky fantasy Trudy has to show her who she belongs to.

The explosive chemistry between them is unmistakable. But will history and geography be obstacles they can't overcome? When Trouble makes a two-week deal with Big Bad...anything can happen.

Warning: **READ THIS!** BDSM, explicit sex, voyeurism, accidental voyeurism, voyeurism OF voyeurism with a sprinkle of m/m, exhibitionism, ropes, cuffs, gratuitous spanking, skinny dipping, irresponsible use of pervertables...and a big, dirty man who will melt your heart.

BILLIONAIRE BACHELORS SERIES

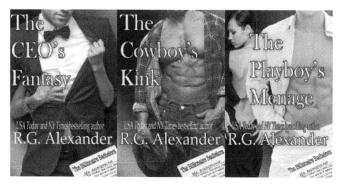

Available Now!
www.RGAlexander.com

Glass slipper shopping can be a dangerous pastime…

The CEO's Fantasy-Book 1

Dean Warren is the billionaire CEO of Warren Industries. He's spent the last five years proving his worth and repairing his family's reputation. But the rules he's had to live by are starting to chafe, especially when it comes to one particular employee. He doesn't believe in coincidence, but when Sara Charles shows up suddenly unemployed and asking him to agree to a month of indulging their most forbidden fantasies--there's no way he can refuse.

When reality is better than his wildest dreams, will the CEO break all of his own rules to keep her?

The Cowboy's Kink-Book 2

Tracy Reyes is a man who enjoys having control. Over his family's billion dollar land and cattle empire, over the women he tops at the club, and over his life. When teacher Alicia Bell drops into his lap with a problem that needs solving and a body that begs to be bound, he can't resist the opportunity to give her the education in kink she needs. But can he walk away from his passionate pupil when it's time to meet his future bride?

The Playboy's Ménage-Book 3

Henry Vincent and Peter Faraday have been friends forever. The royal rocker and polymath playboy have more than a few things in common. They're both billionaires, they both love a challenge...and they've both carried a long-lasting torch for the woman that got away. Finding Holly again brings back feelings and memories neither one of them wanted to face. But they'll have to if they want to share her. Keeping her from running again and making her admit how she feels about them will take teamwork. Hours of teamwork...and handcuffs.

The Bachelors

We know every debutante's mama wants a piece of their action, but if you could choose without repercussions, which of the Billionaire Bachelors would be your fantasy? The true hardcore cowboy who has enough land and employees to start his own country, but no dancing partner for his special kind of two-step? The musician with a royal pedigree, a wild streak and a vast fortune at his disposal, who's never been seen with the same woman twice? His best jet-setting buddy who can claim no less than five estates, four degrees and three charges of lewd public behavior on his record? Or the sweet-talking, picture-perfect tycoon-cum-philanthropist who used to be the baddest of the bunch but put those days behind him when he took over as CEO of his family's company? (Or did he?)

Pick your fantasy lover--rocker, rancher, rebel or reformed rogue. Glass slipper shopping is a dangerous sport to be sure, especially with prey as slippery as these particular animals, but I'll still wish all my readers happy hunting.

From Ms. Anonymous
Available Now!
www.RGAlexander.com

OTHER BOOKS FROM R.G. ALEXANDER

Fireborne Series
Burn With Me
Make Me Burn
Burn Me Down-*coming soon*

Bigger in Texas Series
Big Bad John
Mr. Big Stuff-
Big Trouble-*coming soon*

The Finn Factor Series
Curious
Scandalous
Dangerous
Ravenous-*coming soon*
Shameless-*coming soon*

Billionaire Bachelors Series
The CEO's Fantasy
The Cowboy's Kink
The Playboy's Ménage

Children Of The Goddess Series
Regina In The Sun
Lux In Shadow
Twilight Guardian
Midnight Falls

Wicked Series
Wicked Sexy
Wicked Bad
Wicked Release

Shifting Reality Series
My Shifter Showmance
My Demon Saint

My Vampire Idol

Temptation Unveiled Series
Lifting The Veil
Piercing The Veil
Behind The Veil

Superhero Series
Who Wants To Date A Superhero?
Who Needs Another Superhero?

Kinky Oz Series
Not In Kansas
Surrender Dorothy

Mènage and More
Truly Scrumptious
Three For Me?
Four For Christmas
Dirty Delilah
Marley in Chains

Anthologies
Three Sinful Wishes
Wasteland - Priestess
Who Loves A Superhero?

Bone Daddy Series
Possess Me
Tempt Me
To The Bone

Elemental Steam Series Written As Rachel Grace
Geared For Pleasure

ABOUT R.G. ALEXANDER

R.G. Alexander (aka Rachel Grace) is a *New York Times* and *USA Today* Bestselling author who has written over 30 erotic paranormal, contemporary, sci-fi/fantasy books for multiple e-publishers and Berkley Heat. Both her personalities are represented by the Brown Literary Agency.

She is a founding member of The Smutketeers, an author formed group blog dedicated to promoting fantastic writers, readers and a positive view of female sexuality.

She has lived all over the United States, studied archaeology and mythology, been a nurse, a vocalist, and now a writer who dreams of vampires, witches and airship battles. RG feels lucky every day that she gets to share her stories with her readers, and she loves talking to them on twitter and FB. She is happily married to a man known affectionately as The Cookie—her best friend, research assistant, and the love of her life. Together they battle to tame the wild Rouxgaroux that has taken over their home.

Sign up for the Smutketeers Newsletter
http://eepurl.com/OBKSD
for updates on contest giveaways and
New Releases.
All for Smut and Smut for All!

To Contact R. G. Alexander:
www.RGAlexander.com
www.RachelGraceRomance.com
www.Smutketeers.com
Facebook:
http://www.facebook.com/RachelGrace.RGAlexander
Twitter: https://twitter.com/RG_Alexander

Made in the USA
Charleston, SC
22 August 2015